P9-DDO-821

Antiques
Knock-Off

Also by Barbara Allan:

ANTIQUES ROADKILL

ANTIQUES MAUL

ANTIQUES FLEE MARKET

ANTIQUES BIZARRE

ANTIQUES KNOCK-OFF

By Barbara Collins:

TOO MANY TOMCATS (short story collection)

By Barbara and Max Allan Collins:

REGENERATION

BOMBSHELL

MURDER—HIS AND HERS (short story collection)

Antiques
Knock-Off

A Trash 'n' Treasures Mystery

Barbara Allan

KENSINGTON BOOKS
http://www.kensingtonbooks.com

KENSINGTON BOOKS are published by

Kensington Publishing Corp.
119 West 40th St.
New York, NY 10018

All Kensington titles, imprints, and distributed lines are available at special quantity discounts for bulk purchases for sales promotion, premiums, fund-raising, educational, or institutional use.

Special book excerpts or customized printings can also be created to fit specific needs. For details, write or phone the office of the Kensington Special Sales Manager: Attn. Special Sales Department. Kensington Publishing Corp., 119 West 40th St., New York, NY 10018. Phone: 1-800-221-2647.

Library of Congress Card Catalogue Number: 2010941089

ISBN-13: 978-0-7582-3423-0
ISBN-10: 0-7582-3423-6

First Hardcover Printing: March 2011

10 9 8 7 6 5 4 3 2 1

Printed in the United States of America

In loving memory of William Louis Mull III

Brandy's quote:

Stone walls do not a prison make,
nor iron bars a cage,
Minds innocent and quiet
take that for an hermitage.
Richard Lovelace

Mother's quote:

You can lock me up and throw away the key,
but in my head I'll always be free.
Vivian Borne

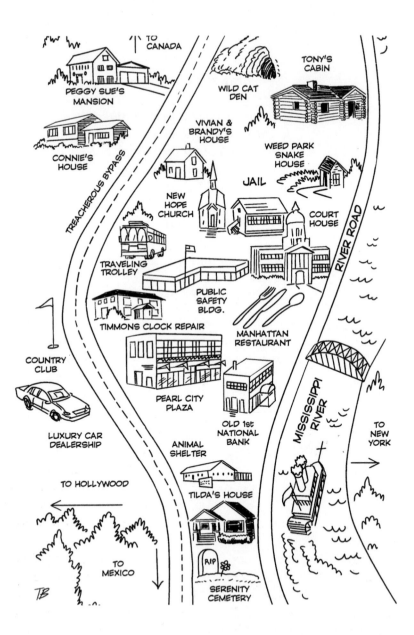

Chapter One

Knock-down

If you are in a bookstore, reading this opening paragraph, trying to decide whether or not to shell out your hard-earned money, you should know that I, Brandy Borne—thirty-one, bottle blonde, divorced, who came running home last year to live with her bipolar mother—am not perfect. I make my share of mistakes. Repeatedly. I am not always what you might call "nice." Nobody's role model.

(Also, there will be parenthetical remarks. I've been told the mark of a really bad writer is the overuse of parenthetical remarks. But you wouldn't know that, if I hadn't made a parenthetical remark just now.)

Therefore, I will understand if you replace this book on the shelf. One favor, please, if you don't make a purchase? Could you face the cover out? And, perhaps (if no clerks are lurking to catch you at it), move the book to a more prominent spot? Thank you.

So much has happened in the fourteen months since I've been back in Serenity, a small Midwestern town nestled on a bend of the mighty Mississippi, that I hardly know where to begin. Actually, I began four books ago, but don't panic—I can catch you up quickly, and those of you who have been with Mother and me from the beginning (God bless you, and no sneeze required) might appreciate a refresher.

Besides the several murder mysteries in which Mother and I got ourselves involved (Mother a willing participant, me not so), I had also received two disturbing anonymous letters.

The first claimed that my much-older sister, Peggy Sue—who lives in a tonier part of town—was my birth mother; the other missive insisted that my biological father was none other than a certain United States senator.

After confronting Sis about these obnoxious notes, she confirmed that their contents were accurate, which put an added strain on our already strained relationship. But we both came to the conclusion that, for the present, we would keep these revelations to ourselves, and not disturb the status quo. Sis was to remain Sis, and Mother Mother... which suited social-climbing Peggy Sue just fine. Me, I had my own reasons for keeping quiet, chief among them not disturbing an already plenty disturbed Mother, who had stopped taking her bipolar medication a few months ago.

We now return you to the regularly scheduled mystery novel (and there *will* be another mystery, and another murder, despite my best efforts otherwise). . . .

Summer had once again arrived in Serenity, though it seemed something of a surprise after endless snow and then continual rain that had caused a flood from which our little community was still recovering. These were what we Midwesterners call the dog days: hot and humid, a literal pressure cooker—well, not a literal pressure cooker, but more than just a figurative one.

And while those with money fled north to Minnesota and Canada until the weather cooled off, we common folk holed up in air-conditioned houses, or malls, or movie theaters, venturing out only in the early-morning hours, or late evening, when the heat was barely tolerable.

At the moment, I was indoors, specifically upstairs in my bedroom, trying to find something to wear that was cool, and *cool*. Because being seven months pregnant during the summer was no picnic.

Oh! Didn't I mention that I was expecting? Sorry. Okay, just a little more catching up. . . .

My best friend, Tina, couldn't have a baby with her husband, Kevin (because she'd had cervical cancer), so I volunteered to be a surrogate mother for them. (Sometimes I *am* nice.) But don't worry—I'm not going to be all, "Ooooh, my back hurts," and "I gotta pee again," for three hundred pages. Nor will you have to encounter such verbs as "trundled," or "waddled." You'll hardly even know I'm preggers. Just, when you picture me—shoulder-length blond hair, blue-eyed, kinda pretty—don't forget to add a baby bump.

From my closet I selected an outfit Tina bought for me—a Juicy Couture yellow sundress (from their maternity line) and a pair of orange Havaianas (flip-flops that I'd always wanted but wouldn't buy myself because I couldn't pronounce them). You see, I figure if you dress right, people won't think "trundle" or "waddle" when you pass them on the street.

Sushi, my brown-and-white, blind, diabetic shih tzu (actually, my only shih tzu, and the only thing besides clothes that I slunk home with after the divorce) (Jake, twelve, was staying with his father in Chicago) (I warned you about the parentheticals) was on the floor a few feet away, attacking an old brown Brighton snakeskin belt as if it were a real reptile. I used the thing to keep her busy while I got dressed, otherwise she'd drag out all my shoes from the closet. I would hide the belt in the bedroom for her to find—which she'd sniff out in a nano-second, even though she couldn't see it, having slobbered on the thing so much.

After checking myself out in the large round mirror of my Art Deco dressing table, feeling a pregnant woman of thirty-one had no right to look so cute, I scooped Sushi up and headed downstairs to find Mother.

This morning, we were taking in an antique mantel clock to be fixed; it was lovely but not keeping time. We had snagged the clock at a tag sale because the seller (an out-of-state relative of the deceased) didn't know its regional value and, naturally, we kept mum, as is the prerogative of any dealer (first rule of collecting).

Mother and I had a booth at the downtown antiques mall—located in a four-story Victorian brick building—and we figured that once the clock had been cleaned and repaired, we could sell it for five times what we paid. Mother would take the lion's share (or lioness's share) because she had spotted it first.

Our acquisition was one of only a few thousand such clocks made right here in Serenity from about 1890 to 1920 by the celebrated Andre Acklin, who had emigrated from Switzerland to take advantage of the top quality wood from our lumber mills (for clock casings), and pearl from the Mississippi mussel shells (clock faces).

As a young man, Acklin had worked in France with Jules Audemars and Edward Piguet—future founders of Audemars Piguet Watch Company—but Acklin went his own way when the other two men began to concentrate on expensive pocket watches. Acklin preferred creating larger timepieces over working in miniature, and also wanted to use more natural materials.

Sadly, Serenity's famed clockmaker died one bitter winter afternoon in 1920, when a fire broke out in his shop on Main Street, blotting out the cold temporarily and the clockmaker permanently. According to local legend, some of his precious inventory did survive.

So, naturally, when Mother and I saw an opportunity to buy an Andre Acklin mantel clock for a song at the tag sale, we were nearly beside ourselves with excitement—although we did our best not to show it (second rule of collecting).

In the kitchen, I found Mother in all her manic glory, standing at the sink, feverishly polishing a vintage silver tea set that we never used. At least her energy, as of late, had been directed toward home improvement, not investigating some murder—real or imagined.

Mother—age unknown because she'd forged so many documents, but who had claimed to be seventy-four for the past three years—was a statuesque Dane, with porcelain skin nearly free of old age spots, wide mouth, narrow nose, prominent cheekbones, and pale blue eyes magnified to twice their size behind large round glasses. She wore her shoulder-length silver-white hair in a variety of buns on a variety of places on her head, even when she went to bed.

Today Mother graced us in a pale yellow blouse and matching capris—one of several new outfits I'd gotten her because she'd lost so much weight during her manic phase, when she slept little and ate even less.

Now, some of you may be asking why I didn't just talk to her about going back on the medication. I did talk. She wouldn't listen.

Why did she refuse to listen to reason? Because, at the age of seventy-whatever, the manic phase makes her feel like Superwoman! She's on a high that can last for months. But then comes the inevitable depression stage (laced with paranoia) and, inevitably—like a jet going three hundred miles an hour at thirty-six-thousand feet—she runs out of gas and nose-dives to Earth.

I just prayed the crash wouldn't happen until after the baby was born.

(I'm not proud of this, but I tried crushing one of her pills and hiding it in her favorite pastry—a vanilla cream-horn—but she caught on with one bite, and threw the rest of the pastry—and her medicine—away.) (This technique doesn't work on Sushi, either.)

"If you don't stop doing that," I said, "you'll polish the silver right off."

Mother held the teapot out by its ornate handle, saying proudly, "Look, dear, I can see my face in it!"

So could I, a funhouse reflection with giant bug eyes, and I could only wonder if it was how she viewed the world at the moment—recognizable, if distorted.

"Mother," I said, "we should hurry—before it gets too hot out."

"Oh, yes, dear," she said with a pensive frown. "The clock." She set the teapot down and began wiping her hands with a dishtowel. "You've packed it well?"

I nodded.

"What about Sushi? Do you think the little doggie would like to go with us?"

"Moth-er," I groaned.

Groaned, because at the mention of her name, Sushi would no doubt come running, and did. That and the word "go" had her dancing at our feet.

"Oh, I *am* sorry," Mother said. "The little devil knows the word 'go,' doesn't she? I should have *spelled* 'go,' instead of *said* 'go.' "

"Will you please stop *saying* 'go'?"

Sushi was in a frenzy now, yapping ever louder.

Mother put hands on hips. "Now *you* just said, 'go.' "

"There you go *again!*"

We glared at each other in what was an all-too-common

occurrence around the Borne homestead: a stalemate of idiocy.

I sighed. "Well, now, she'll *have* to go with us."

"I guess she will," Mother huffed, "because *you* keep saying 'go.' "

I left (*not* trundled!) to get the dog carrier in the front closet, Sushi underfoot, almost making me trip. Normally, I enjoyed taking Soosh out with me on short errands, but this time we were going to a new place—Timmons Clock Repair—and I didn't know if there would be another dog on the premises, or how long we would stay . . . and, besides, we were toting along a valuable antique.

But now, if we didn't take Sushi, the little furball would surely exact her revenge, and that could mean (but would necessarily not be limited to) any of the following: peeing on the Oriental rug, chewing the leg / arm of a Queen Anne chair, tearing up a feather pillow, unrolling the toilet paper. Barricading the blind barker in the kitchen never worked—the one and only time we did that, she chewed off all the corners of the lower cabinets.

I did own a rhinestone-studded dog-carrying bag, but the pink balboa feathers made Sushi sneeze, so I'd replaced the bag with a baby front-pack (pink, pictured with rattles and pacifiers and diaper pins), which was better because it freed up my hands.

I had just strapped the front-pack on and was preparing to deal with the dog, when the doorbell rang. Our postwoman—short brown hair, no make-up, athletic build—handed me the mail and, after exchanging a few words with her about how hot it was, I closed the door, then put the correspondence on a nearby Victorian marble-top table reserved for such things as car keys, loose change, sunglasses, cell phones, and grocery lists.

I'd been waiting for a rebate check on my new phone—

which I intended on blowing on the end-of-summer shoe sales, because shoes would still fit after the baby came—so I took the time to sift through the mail.

Electric bill, water bill, church bulletin, *You-Could-Win-a-Million-Dollars!* notice, letter with no return address, phone bill, fashion magazine . . .

. . . *letter with no return address!*

I snatched up the familiar white envelope with distinctive computer font, but was surprised this time to see it addressed to . . . Vivian Borne.

Mother.

And she was right there, instantly suspicious. "What is that you have there, dear?"

I whirled, hiding the anonymous letter behind my back.

"Nothing. Just more junk mail." And I laughed a little, in that unconvincing way the guilty do in movies.

Mother's eyes narrowed, her voice taking on a strange, dubious tone. "If it's *nothing,* dear, why *conceal* it?"

I was in a kerfuffle—should I lie about the letter, and increase her paranoia? Or give it to her, knowing its contents might well send her on a downward spiral? Not the best of options. . . .

I handed the letter over, with a "You're not going to like it" look.

She ignored that, and strode over to her favorite Queen Anne needlepoint armchair, and sat regally, while I crossed the Oriental rug to the matching needlepoint sofa, settling as comfortably as I could on the rigid furniture.

I watched with increasing anxiety as Mother opened the envelope, unfolded the single-sheet contents, then brought it up closer to her glasses.

Sushi, sensing a postponement in our trip, found a stream of sunlight to swim in, placing her head on her crossed front paws, her lower lip protruding poutily.

I could pretty much guess what the letter said, going by

the two I'd already received. But as Mother slowly read it aloud, I clearly had underestimated the depth and scope of viciousness intended by its sender.

" 'Soon all will know that Brandy is not your daughter,' " Mother said, then paused, realizing what had just come out of her. Then she resumed, in an atypically hushed voice. " '. . . and that Peggy Sue is her real mother. And Senator Clark can kiss his political career good-bye.' "

Mother's hand containing the letter dropped to her lap, her face turning ashen; then a bright red burn began at her neck, working its way up.

She turned to me, eyes blazing. "You *knew?*"

I nodded.

"How *long* have you known?"

I shrugged, as if I were the one who'd wrongly withheld a secret. "A few months. First one I got was about Peggy Sue. Second one was about Senator Clark."

"And Peggy Sue? She *knows* that . . . *you* know?"

I nodded again. "She got her own nice anonymous notes."

Mother stood, pointing at me, *j'accuse.* "And *you* kept this from me? How could you *do* such a thing?"

"Hey! *You* kept it from *me* for thirty years! So don't get up on your high horse."

Mother stared for a long moment, then nodded. Her manner was disturbingly calm. "Point well taken, my dear. You have a perfect right to be miffed."

"*Miffed?*"

"But you must understand . . . we did what we thought was best."

"Best for *whom*, Mother? You and Peggy Sue, you mean?"

Mother came to join me on the couch, putting one hand on my knee. "No, Brandy . . . best for you. Peggy Sue couldn't have cared for a baby properly—she was only eighteen, and unmarried—times were so different back then. And since the man you thought of as your father— my husband, Jonathan Borne—had just died, you gave me great comfort." Her eyes seemed about to overflow. "Did . . . did I do such a bad job, dear?"

I had already thought about that. "No, Mother. Life with Peggy Sue would have been pretty dull compared to living with you."

After all, would Sis have pulled me out of school when I was seven, to try her luck on Broadway? (Mother only made off-off-off Broadway. Off-off-off meaning the Newark Community Playhouse.)

Or would Peggy Sue have been chased through a corn-field by the county sheriff with commitment papers, and me bouncing around in the back seat of the car? Not likely.

Those were the makings of, if not exactly *fond* memo-ries, certainly vivid ones.

Mother was saying, "Remember, dear, that at that time Peggy Sue was in no position to give you the kind of luxu-rious life she could later afford to provide her own daugh-ter, Ashley. She was only able to do all that by completing college, and snagging a good husband like Bob."

I said, "I know."

I'd been all through that little exercise with my thera-pist, Cynthia Hays. And I didn't care to revisit it.

"Are we . . . all right, dear? Have we changed, you and I?"

I allowed my eyes to meet her exaggerated ones behind the lenses. "I'm not sure either one of us is capable of much change, Mother. I'm always content with just not re-gressing."

"I mean, darling . . . am I still your mother? Am I still *Mother?* I think it would just kill me if you began calling me . . . calling me . . ."

I put a finger to her lips. "Mother. Always Mother."

Not Grandma. Not now. Not at this late date.

Mother gave me a hug and I hugged her back. Then she sighed and stood, and went to retrieve the fallen letter.

"Who do you think sent this?" she asked, waving the paper in one hand, an angry prosecutor flinging evidence at the jury.

"My money's on Connie Grimes."

Mother blinked owlishly. "Peggy Sue's good friend?"

"Peggy Sue's *so-called* 'good friend.' "

Mother frowned in thought, then went to the picture window and gazed out, her back to me.

After a long moment she turned dramatically. Make that melodramatically.

"Yes," she said slowly. "I do believe you're right, dear. The little witch has always been jealous of Peggy Sue. . . ."

"That's witch with a *b,* Mother. And it's a long time since she's been 'little.' "

". . . and after all, you *did* throw her down the escalator at Ingram's Department Store last fall!"

"No, I didn't!" I held my head high. "All I did was push her into a display of Halloween sweaters." After she had called Mother and me crazy. "It was a soft enough landing."

Mother looked disappointed, clearly liking the other version better. "Oh, I've been telling everyone it was the escalator. Well, no matter . . . the Grimes woman *is* the likely candidate for wanting to cause trouble for all of us."

Mother's use of the word "candidate" put me back on point. I asked, "Did Connie work on Senator Clark's campaign along with Peggy Sue?"

Mother qualified her nod. "But she didn't go on the campaign trail, like your . . . sister." She paused, adding, "That's when you were conceived, dear."

I grunted. "I hope in a five-star hotel, and not the back of a campaign bus."

"It was, dear. The Drake in Chicago."

I smirked. "Sis always does go first-class."

Mother wadded up the letter in an angry, shaking fist. "The question is—what can we *do* about that horrible woman?"

"What about Mr. Ekhardt?" I asked. "Could he send her a cease-and-desist?"

Wayne Cyrus Ekhardt had been our family attorney since long before I was born. Now a spry if somewhat snoozy ninety, Ekhardt still kept an office downtown, with limited hours, and only a handful of clients, us among them.

Mother said, "I'm afraid not, dear—not unless we have *definite* proof she is the culprit. If we have Wayne send her a threatening letter, she could turn around and sue us for false claim!"

I shook my head, burning. "And she'd do it, too."

Mother returned to nestle next to me on the couch, sweeping a loose strand of hair away from my face, then patting it back into place.

"Now don't you worry your pretty little head about this," she soothed. "Mother will take of it."

"That's what I'm *afraid* of. . . ."

Mother arched an eyebrow. "And what do you *think* I'm going to do?"

"Well, I don't suppose you'd kill Connie. . . . Would you?"

"Oh ye of little faith," Mother said with a shake of her head. "*You* know very well which side of murder cases I come down on. . . . Why, all I'm going to do is apply the tactic of our president—*talk* to the enemy. Open a line of communication." She slapped her knees like a department store Santa summoning the next brat. "Now!

We best go on our antiquing errand before the heat sets in."

Sushi, previously prone in a depressed puddle, now snapped to attention, and when my rise from the couch confirmed our eminent departure, the pooch began running in circles, as if chasing her tail—which was unlikely, since she couldn't see it.

A few minutes later I was behind the wheel of my gently battered burgundy Buick, Mother beside me, holding Sushi on her lap, three Musketeers heading to the clock repair shop. One for all and all for Mother.

While tooling along Mulberry Street—a main artery to the downtown—an all-too-common occurrence happened: Mother suddenly sat forward and yelled, *"Stop!"*

Any other driver might have thought a child had run into the street chasing a ball, or a dog had chosen an unfortunate time to cross the road, or perhaps a despondent squirrel had picked that moment to commit vehicular hara-kiri . . .

. . . but, since it was garbage collection day along Mulberry Street, I knew Mother had merely spotted something with her magnified eyes that she had decided simply *must* be salvaged.

Dutifully, I pulled over—ours not to reason why and so on. Mother passed Sushi to me, hopped out of the car and scurried back to a pile of junk at the curb. Moments later, she returned, put her find in the back seat beside our boxed clock, then resumed her position in the rider's seat.

I looked over my shoulder at the dirty old coal bucket and said, "It has a hole in it."

Mother, taking Sushi back onto her lap, scoffed, "All buckets have holes in them, dear."

"Not in the side."

"That can be fixed." She pointed windshield-ward. "Forward ho, dear."

Great. Now we had yet another addition to an entire garage filled with things that could be fixed—none of which, so far anyway, had been.

(*Aside:* Unbeknownst to Mother, I had gradually been throwing out her trashy treasures on *our* garbage day. Wait a minute! She'll read this and know. . . .)

Note to editor: please strike above paragraph if I haven't cleared everything out of the garage by day of publication.

Onward to the downtown. . . .

Over the past decade, Serenity—population twenty-five thousand (give or take a few hundred)—had reinvented itself from a middle-class river town (founded in the mid-1800s) to an upscale tourist destination, touting antique stores, specialty shops, and bistros.

Giving the devil her due, Mother had played a major role in the transformation, after an entire block—which included the lovely old brick YWCA, the Art Deco movie house, and a Victorian ice cream parlor—had been mercilessly leveled to make way for a parking lot.

When she made bail, after chaining herself to the wrecking ball, Mother formed the Serenity Architectural Preservation Society (SAPS)—she did admit, some weeks later, that she might have paid better attention to the initials. I suggested the group instead become the Association of Community Resources Organized to Nurture Your Municipality (ACRONYM). But Mother didn't get the joke.

Anyway, SAPS set out to prevent any further destruction of the town's heritage, and gradually, one by one, the dilapidated buildings were restored to their former glory, if rarely to their original purposes.

Timmons Clock Repair was located on Fourth Street at the end of the downtown grid, in a large gray stucco building that had once been a rather grand funeral home. Ben Timmons owned the pseudo-mansion, renting out its many downstairs rooms to other proprietors selling wares that complemented his clock repair business, such as up-scale antiques, choice vintage clothing, and wood refinishing.

The only thing creepy about the place—other than its phony facades and fake balconies, which lent an admittedly eerie aura of unreality—was that the clock repair shop was housed in the one-time preparation room, where Timmons blithely used the ancient embalming tables as workbenches.

I parked the car in a side lot and we got out, Mother handing Sushi over to me to put in my front carry-on, while she retrieved the boxed Acklin mantel clock.

As we were heading up a walk lined with red geraniums, Mrs. Vancamp, an old friend of Mother's, trotted out of the building toward us. The former high school counselor—who once told me I'd never amount to much, so I guess she was right—was a diminutive woman with bird-like features and nervous, quick movements to match. Coincidentally, she wore a cotton housedress with red robins on it. She had better eyesight than Mr. Magoo, but barely.

As evidenced by her opening remark: "Oh, Brandy! I see you've had your *baby*—is it a girl?"

Mrs. Vancamp appeared to be looking at Sushi, through glasses thicker than Mother's, although Mrs. Vancamp's glasses made her eyes really, really tiny, like dried-up raisins.

I smiled politely. "Yes, it's a girl."

"*Ohhh* . . . isn't she *adorable*," the woman cooed, adding, "and just *look* at all that *hair!*"

Mother was ignoring that bit of unintentional buffoonery, focusing on the sack in Mrs. Vancamp's hands. "What do you have there, Cora?"

The woman beamed. "I simply *must* show you! I just had it cleaned." From the sack she carefully withdrew a small bedside table clock. "My husband bought it for me just before he died—it's an *Acklin*, of course—and it gives me such comfort in the morning when I wake up . . . almost as if Harry were still beside me, ticking instead of snoring."

Mother peered closer. "Yes, dear. That *is* nice. . . ."

Whether Mother was referring to the clock she was examining or the mention of Cora's late husband was unclear.

But Mrs. Vancamp asked for no clarification, as she rewrapped her treasure. "Well, girls, I must be going—I have other errands to run before it gets too darned hot, as the kids say."

"Kids" who said that were Mother's age.

Mrs. Vancamp's minuscule eyes traveled to my stomach, which was pooching out below my pooch. "Don't despair, dear—your figure will come back, eventually. Just more of it!"

She then moved past us, heading toward the parking lot.

As we stood for a moment watching her, Mother murmured, "If *that's* an Acklin, I'll eat my Red-Hatted League hat."

Which I would have paid to see, because that particular chapeau was as big as a hubcap, albeit a hubcap encrusted with red rhinestones and purple feathers.

"It looked authentic to me," I said.

"Acklin *never* used oak."

"Oh. Well, I'm no expert. So, then, it's a knock-off?" Pause. "*Mother. . . .*"

"Yes, dear, a knock-off."

"No, Mother. What I mean to say is . . . Mrs. Vancamp?"

"Yes, dear?"

"She's getting in a *car*."

"Your point being?"

"Behind the wheel."

Mother sighed. "I know—it's outrageous, isn't it? A woman with her poor eyesight is allowed to drive and yet a woman with my driving skills and *perfect* eyesight and razor-sharp reactions has her license taken away!"

My mother had a driving record the way John Dillinger had a banking record. Her most recent, unlicensed episode involved running down a mailbox. But I restrained myself, mostly because I was gaping at Mrs. Magoo stop-starting her way out of the former funeral home's lot.

Even Mother seemed alarmed. "We'd best linger inside a while, until she's off the streets. Cora always was a terrible driver, even before the glaucoma."

We entered the old funeral home, then moved down a faded floral-carpeted hallway off of which four large rooms (two to a side) with arched doorways yawned.

In days gone by, the rooms had served as separate grieving parlors, not thriving shops. A few telltale indications of their original intent remained, such as the overuse of small alcoves for urns and churchlike stained-glass windows.

Timmons Clock Repair was at the end of the hallway, beyond a pebble-glass door on which the faint outline of PREPARATION ROOM bled through the current business's name. We stepped inside.

Another creepy funeral home reminder greeted us—affixed to the back / front walls were ancient embalming paraphernalia, including black rubber hoses and preparation tools, sort of like the way a country-style restaurant might display small antique farm implements.

A long counter bisected the room, separating us from Ben Timmons, bent over a former embalming table, doing an autopsy on a clock. He'd heard our entrance, and as we approached, he straightened, pushed a magnifying eyepiece to his forehead like a third eye, and came forward.

Timmons, in his mid to late fifties, was a short, compact man, with a blossoming middle-age spread, salt-and-pepper hair, all-salt beard, and pleasant features. He wore a suit, or anyway the vest and pants of one, his sleeves rolled up, a red bow tie giving him a crisp look. He had the demeanor of someone who was doing the kind of work that he loved. Nothing funeral-home creepy about him at all.

He asked with a smile, "What brings you inside on this lovely day, ladies?"

Apparently he hadn't heard about the heat wave.

Mother, who had placed our boxed clock on the counter, leaned toward our pleasant host with a narrow-eyed glare. "I just saw Mrs. Vancamp outside . . . and she *thinks* her clock is an *Acklin!*"

My Prozac-free mind (I'd been off the little capsules since getting pregnant) began to register anxiety at Mother's confrontational tone.

Two of Timmons's three eyes briefly looked downward, then back to meet Mother's. "Yes, Mrs. Borne, poor Mrs. Vancamp *does* believe the clock is authentic. And, of course, it isn't."

Mother drew herself up. "*How* could you not *tell* 'poor Mrs. Vancamp,' Ben?" Vivian Borne was on a first-name basis with everyone. "Don't you have *some* sense of ethical responsibility?"

Timmons took a moment to answer. "Actually, I do. But sometimes it's not as easy as you might think. Did Mrs. Vancamp explain how she got the clock?"

"Well . . . *yes,*" Mother said, irked at the dodging of her question. "She said her husband bought it, just before he died."

"Supposedly," he responded coolly.

Mother's frown deepened. "And what does 'supposedly' mean?"

While I stood by silently, the clocksmith explained that Mrs. Vancamp had told him an antiques dealer called her a few days after the funeral, saying her husband had put a down payment on an Acklin clock intended as a sixtieth wedding anniversary present. Did she still want the clock? Of, course, the balance of a thousand dollars would be due.

Mother and I exchanged sickened looks. This type of scam was one of the vilest, preying upon the sentiments of the bereaved at a vulnerable time. Usually, however, the merchandise—often diamonds or other valuable jewelry—was authentic, to keep the seller out of trouble. But the scam perpetrated on Mrs. Vancamp had taken another, nasty twist: the merchandise was fake.

I asked, "Did Mrs. Vancamp mention who sold her the clock?"

Timmons nodded. "And there's no such person. I checked. The creep even used a phony post office box on the receipt."

Mother's manner softened. "I'm afraid I wouldn't have had the heart to tell her, either, Ben. Luckily, since her eyesight is so bad, I doubt she'll ever be the wiser."

"Unless she tries to sell it," I pointed out.

Timmons said, "Mrs. Vancamp wouldn't likely ever do that—that clock means too much to her. But, if she ever should, I'm sure she'll come to me for an estimate . . . and then I guess I'll have to come clean."

"I can live with that," Mother said crisply, as if her consent was needed.

Timmons looked at our box. "Now—what have you here?"

"Well, Ben," Mother said with an only slightly demented smile, "unlike Mrs. Vancamp, *we* have the real *thing!*"

She opened our parcel, removed the bubble-pack, and placed the mantel clock on the counter.

Timmons moved his third eye down over his right one, and examined our find, carefully turning it over, then checked the inner workings.

Finally, he said with some excitement, "Yes, you have! And it's in *beautiful* condition! Do you mind telling me where you got it?"

Mother did. In excruciating detail.

"Well, it's a lucky find," Timmons granted. "I know you girls are really into antiques, and this would make a wonderful addition to your collection, really would make a fine showpiece for your home. What are you going to do with it?"

"I think we'll probably hang on to it," I said, not wanting to tip our hand. "Providing you can make it keep time. And we'll need an estimate, first."

Timmons was about to respond when the pebble-glass door opened, then banged shut with such force that Mother and I turned around, startled.

Connie Grimes was as taken aback to see us as we were her. The middle-aged, mousy-haired matron wore a voluminous blue linen tent dress that tried but failed to hide her heft, a "little" number I recognized from Eileen Fisher's new spring line. Quickly, the woman's surprised expression turned to disdain.

"Well," she said with a sneer, "I'd ask what you were doing here, Vivian, but I'd imagine you're an expert on *cuckoo* clocks."

I moved toward her, Sushi growling in her pouch. "Leave my mother alone."

Her eyes flared. "Stay away from me, and the mongrel, too!"

" *'And your little dog, too!'* " I mocked.

Her nostrils flared. "That restraining order is still in effect, remember!"

"Maybe the judge would be interested in seeing some interesting notes Mother, Peggy Sue, and I have been receiving. Maybe he'd like to hear all about our poisoned-pen pal."

Connie's face, which had once been pretty but now wore fat in random globs, like clay misplaced by a careless sculptor, tightened into a nasty smile. "There's no law against sending unsigned letters."

"There's a law against libel."

"And *truth* is the best defense, isn't it? Why don't you two run along? I have some private business to discuss with Mr. Timmons. Surely there's something you and your mother could do together, to pass a few minutes—or should I say *grandmother?*"

I had never seen Mother move so quickly—except maybe when she had spotted the Acklin clock—and before I could do anything except get out of her path, she'd flown at Connie like an oversized avenging bird, pushing the woman back against the wall of artifacts where Connie got tangled up in the antique embalming hoses.

Sushi squirmed out of the baby carrier, leaping from my chest to the floor, and—blindness be damned—rushed to protect Mother by sinking her sharp little teeth into Connie—well, not Connie, but her new linen dress, making ripping tears . . . because Soosh really knew how to hurt a girl.

Ben Timmons rushed around the counter to break up the altercation, which he accomplished by latching on to Mother's arms and pulling her away from Connie.

Casting off the black hoses like deadly asps, the middle-aged Medusa screamed at Mother, "You're going to pay *dearly* for that, you crazy old crone!" To Timmons, Connie shrilled, "Call the police! *Right now!* You saw what happened—that nutcase *attacked* me! It's assault and battery! *Do* it!"

To which Timmons replied, "I'm afraid, Mrs. Grimes, what I saw was you tripping and falling against the wall."

Connie's face reddened further. "So *that's* how it's going to be? You're going to stick up for *them,* after cheating *me?* Well, you won't get away with it! I'm going straight to my lawyer. . . ."

She whirled and tromped out, slamming the door again, rattling the glass.

Mother was smoothing out her sleeves where Timmons had gripped her, gathering the shreds of her dignity.

"Whew!" Timmons said, with a roll of his eyes. "That's one customer I don't mind losing."

"What was that about you cheating her?" I asked.

He shrugged. "The contentious Mrs. Grimes claims I overcharged her for a repair. I didn't. Some people think they deserve special rates."

"She deserves *something,*" I said. I was shaken up, but hadn't realized it till it was over.

Mother said, "Thank you, Ben, for what you did. . . ."

I voiced my appreciation, too. Mother could have landed in the county jail for that; in truth, she *had* attacked the woman. God bless her.

"Don't mention it," Timmons said with a smile. "Now. Why don't two you go on home, and I'll call you later with an estimate on your clock."

As Mother and I walked down the long hallway, I asked, "What happened to using the tactics of our president—*talk* to the enemy and so on?"

"Well, dear," Mother replied, "I decided to take the advice of a *different* president."

"Which one?"

"T.R., dear. T.R."

"Oh?"

"Walk softly," she said with a chuckle, "but carry a big stick."

But I wasn't laughing. Connie Grimes would most certainly ramp up her attack on us.

I muttered, "She's lucky somebody doesn't kill her."

"Look on the bright side, dear," Mother said cheerfully. "Maybe someone will."

A Trash 'n' Treasures Tip

With modern technology, fake antiques can be found among furniture, pottery, glassware, photographs, metalworks, and every other area of collecting. Even a skilled collector can sometimes be fooled. To protect yourself, become knowledgeable in your field of interest. For example, I know everything there is to know about smiley-face clocks.

Chapter Two

Knocked-off

Peggy Sue lived in an expensive home in a new subdivision on the outskirts of Serenity, along with husband Bob, and Ashley, her only child (not counting me).

Bob, who ran his own accounting firm, was a workaholic—not by choice but necessity, thanks to Sis's extravagant tastes. Ashley, a sophomore in college, attended an exclusive private school in the East and, even though spoiled rotten, she had Borne spunk in her DNA, which kept me from resenting her utterly for getting the soft, cushy life that might have been mine.

After the incident between Mother and Connie Grimes at the clock repair shop, I had called Peggy Sue to say I needed to see her, but didn't want to go into details over the phone. We set up a time in the early evening, when Mother would be gone, rehearsing at the Playhouse for her upcoming community production, in which she would don dual hats as director and lead actress in *Opal Is a Diamond*.

(*Note one:* Referring to her role as the eccentric, garbage-collecting Opal, Mother had commented, "I'll have to stretch my veteran acting chops to pull *this* part off.")

(*Note two:* When I went to the first rehearsal, I found director-Mother yelling at actress-Mother, "You're playing that too *broadly*, Vivian," and actress-Mother yelling at director-Mother, "You don't know *what* you're talking about, Vivian!" I vowed to stay away until opening night.)

Around seven P.M., I pulled my battered Buick up the long wide concrete driveway to the triple garage of Peggy Sue's monstrous three-story brick mansion. All inhabitants were home, apparently—the garage door was open, showing off Bob's flashy silver BMW sports car, Sis's blue Cadillac Escalade, and Ashley's red Mustang convertible.

When I turned off my car, the engine knocked, and the tailpipe backfired a big ol' car fart, giving me a perverse pleasure because the ruckus drew disapproving stares from a few snooty neighbors out in their picture-perfect yards. (Phew! I think that's the longest sentence I ever wrote.)

Then up the yellow brick road to Emerald City skipped little me, to ring the bell. To my surprise, Ashley opened the door.

"I thought you were off at college," I said.

Ashley was a beauty, and I had only admiration and not the tiniest twinge of resentment for her tall and slender form, set off by Peggy Sue's auburn hair, only worn sleek and straight. My niece / secret-half-sis was prepped-out in a lavender Lacoste polo shirt, white shorts, and pink Puma canvas sneakers.

"No college till next week," Ashley said, flashing white, perfect teeth. Okay, those I resented her for. She reached out and patted my tummy. "How's the pregnancy?"

"Comin' down the pike," I said with a grin. "Just two more months."

"Boy, you don't look it!"

"You're officially my favorite niece."

"And your only niece." She drew back and made room.

I stepped into the foyer, saying, "Now, doesn't that feel good," the air-conditioning welcoming me with out-stretched arms.

As Ashley closed the door, she began, "Aunt Brandy, I was wondering . . ."

I turned to face her.

". . . since I'm not taking my car to college, would you like to drive it while I'm gone? Otherwise, it's just gonna sit useless in the garage."

For a moment, I saw myself behind the wheel, tooling along the highways and byways, top down (the car, not me!). But then I envisioned Mother sneaking out, helping herself to the snazzy wheels with her bad eyesight and no driver's license to make a midnight run to Walmart for chocolate mint ice cream . . . and getting stopped by the cops.

Who, at this point, would likely lock her up and throw away the key.

But was that a *bad* thing?

My thoughtful frown prompted Ashley to say, "It's okay with Mom and Dad. I already asked."

"It's not that, Ash," I replied. "I'd feel just terrible if something happened to it." I smiled and touched her arm, "But thanks, anyway. . . . It's really sweet of you to offer."

A good kid. Here she was, instinctively treating me like a big sister when as far as she knew, I was just her lowly aunt.

As I proceeded down the gleaming blond-wood hall-way—Ashley heading upstairs with a little wave and a wink—Bob stepped out of the side room that he used as his office-away-from-the-office.

I greeted him with, "Well, don't *you* look tanned and rested." He and Sis had just taken a much-overdue vaca-tion to Hawaii.

"I don't know about 'rested,' " he said with an easy

smile. "You know how your sister is—she ran me ragged, sightseeing."

Even factoring in Peggy Sue's ability to make having fun an onerous task, my comment had been a half-truth: Bob was tanned, but obviously anything but rested, appearing far older than his fifty or so, hair thinner, eyes more hollow, slender frame hanging off stooped shoulders.

As far as I was concerned, he was working himself to death for the love—and contentment—of my sister. The poor dumb slob.

"Hey, you don't look so bad yourself," he said. "Must be that fabled pregnancy glow we hear so much about!"

I smirked. "Any glow I have's from being baked in the heat, Bob . . . or maybe half-baked. But thanks—a girl seven months along loves a compliment. Uh, say, uh . . . Bob . . . ?"

"Yes?"

"If I'm stepping over the line, into confidential business stuff, just stop me."

"Go ahead. If you are, I will."

"Okay. Don't Connie Grimes and her husband have some investments with you?"

"Yes. . . ." His tone was guarded, and he looked puzzled. "But you're right that I can't tell you anything more than that."

"That's all I want to know. See, Mother and Connie had a little . . . run-in . . . ."

"Run-in? How little?"

"Sort of a shoving match. Kind of one-sided. On Mother's side."

His eyebrows went up, then down. "Oh. I see."

"And if we can't get it straightened out . . . maybe you could have a little talk with Connie? Ask her to back off, and maybe forget about it? I have this little, uh, restraining order where Connie is concerned, and then naturally Mother really can't afford to get in any more legal jams."

He was frowning in thought. "I get you. But, Brandy—we're not really close, Connie and me . . . and I haven't done any business with either her or her husband since they first invested, and that was a while ago."

"Oh. Well. Sure. I understand."

He melted. Peggy Sue must have seen that expression a million times. "But look, of course I will try—only maybe you and Peg could work to settle the thing with her, first."

"Fair enough, Bob. Thanks. Sorry to impose."

"No imposition. Anything for my best girl's baby sister." He gestured down the hallway. "And you'll find my best girl in the kitchen."

I hugged him, as much as my baby bump would allow anyway, and he patted my back like I was the baby and this was a burping session. Then he ducked back into his office.

I found Sis towel-drying off a few dishes at an island counter that had its own sink and glass top burners, just in case the nearby double sink and enormous stove couldn't accommodate a family of three.

Barely granting me a glance, Peg said, "I have a DAR meeting in half an hour, so make it quick."

Peggy Sue belonged to the Daughters of the American Revolution, and would lead you to believe that the distant ancestor who qualified her to join had fought bravely and with distinction in the War of Independence. But actually (I did my own on-line research) he had been pressed into service at gunpoint and later hanged as a horse thief.

But who's quibbling?

I took a deep breath. "I know you're busy, but this is important. You know I don't just drop by without a reason."

Peggy Sue glanced again, sharply this time. "I've noticed. What is it?"

"It's Connie."

Her eyes rolled. "Why can't you two just peacefully co-exist?"

"Because she broke the non-proliferation treaty and went nuclear."

My lovely sister sighed. "Must *everything* be a major melodrama with you?"

"You decide if I'm exaggerating. Connie sent Mother an anonymous letter, so now Mother knows everything."

Peggy Sue set down a dish almost hard enough to break; hard enough to clatter on that perfect counter. Her expression was stricken.

I went on. "Then we went cheerfully to the clock repair shop, where Connie happened to show up and Mother attacked her . . ."

"*What?*"

". . . and Mr. Timmons had to break it up and Connie told him to call the police but he said all he saw was Connie tripping on her own big feet, and that made her madder, naturally, and now she's going to sue our behinds. *What?* You said make it quick."

Sis was glaring, her brown eyes flashing. Then, in a rare show of temper, the ice queen whapped her dish towel against the island counter.

"You bring news like *this,*" she fumed, "and make a joke out of it?"

I shrugged. "We laugh so as not to cry. But either way, the cat is *well* out of the bag, and we had all better prepare for the kind of storm that comes down very, very brown."

The anger evaporated from her face, and so did the blood. "But . . . but I thought this had gone *away.*" It was a whine. "And Connie was so *nice* to me at bridge club the other day, and then again at . . ."

I snorted. "Don't you get it? That nutzoid bitch is toying with you."

"I don't like that kind of language."

"What—nutzoid? Peggy Sue—Connie will *never* give up. And if Mother received a letter, you can bet Senator Clark got one too."

A perfectly manicured hand flew like a wounded bird and perched at my sister's pretty mouth. "Oh, God . . ." Her porcelain face somehow turned even whiter, as she leaned against the counter. "Dear God . . ."

"I take it you haven't told Bob and Ashley about us and Senator Clark yet. Coming in, I saw them both and nothing in their behavior indicated I was anything to them but plain old preggers Auntie."

She shook her head, the arcs of her auburn pageboy swinging against her pale cheeks.

"Sis? You okay?"

Suddenly she straightened, her troubled eyes struggling to find hope. "Maybe . . . maybe *I* can talk to Connie—you know . . . convince her to stop. Before it's too late."

"It *is* too late," I said flatly. "You and I need to come out of the mother / daughter closet. Otherwise, you stand to be emotionally blackmailed for the rest of your life. Time to come clean."

"But Bob . . . and Ashley . . ."

"Those two love you beyond reason. They would stand by you if you *murdered* that cow, and I wouldn't blame you if you did."

Peggy Sue looked crushed, her eyes filling with tears.

I went to her, put a hand on her shoulder. "Look, Sis . . . why don't *I* pay a visit to the Wicked Witch of the Midwest tomorrow morning, and talk to her?"

"What about the restraining order?"

"That will give her the upper hand, and she'll love it. Let me at least see if she's planning a lawsuit against

Mother. I will tell her we'll forget all about the poisoned pen letters if she'll forget about Mother pushing her. Then you can talk to her, and maybe reason with her."

Sis nodded numbly.

"In the meantime, you'd better fill Bob in. . . ." I turned to leave, then looked back. "By the way . . . what ever did you do to Connie to deserve this kind of treatment?"

"Nothing! Nothing serious."

"That sounds like something."

She shrugged. "You may find this hard to believe, but Connie was really very beautiful in high school. She was a cheerleader, and part of the Homecoming Queen court."

"When you were Homecoming Queen, you mean."

"Yes. I didn't really get serious with Bob till college, but, uh . . . I dated him in high school for several months, my junior year."

"Why is that important?"

"It isn't." Peggy Sue's smile was brittle, like very thin ice. "I sort of . . . stole Bob away from her. But who carries around that kind of high-school baggage into adulthood?"

I just shrugged and said my good-byes, thinking about how a fling with an old flame at my high school ten-year reunion had ended a marriage.

Mine.

By eight that evening, I had left Peggy Sue's and was heading for Tina and Kevin's house. I felt it was time to bring them into the mix, not wanting my BFF and her husband to hear Connie's scuttlebutt from any scuttle but me.

The couple lived just north of town in a white ranch-style house on a bluff overlooking the mighty Mississippi. I had cell-phoned ahead to make sure they were home, keeping my voice calm and friendly, because with me in the last trimester, they had become very jumpy expectant parents.

All I had to do was call and say, "Hi," and I got, "Are you all right? Brandy, is everything all right? We're on our way! Don't panic! Everything will be fine!" (I didn't specify whether that was more likely to be Tina or Kevin, because it could have been either.)

The setting sun was sending brilliant pink rays darting through the trees as I tooled along the two-lane blacktop to their house, where I found Tina and Kevin sitting on the porch in matching white wicker rockers. As I pulled in, they stood and moved in tandem to the edge of the porch, Kevin slipping an arm around Tina.

Teen was a year older than me, slender, with natural blond hair and blue eyes. We had become BFF's in high school, when some snooty senior girls were picking on her in the hallway, and I came around the corner and tore them all a new one. *(Editor: Can I say that?)* We had a fun year together at community college, then I escaped home (and Mother) by marrying a hunky thirty-year-old investment banker named Roger, and moving to a suburban utopia near Chicago. Meanwhile, Tina snagged Kevin and stayed put in Serenity, working at the tourism department, while her hubby sold pharmaceuticals. Now they were both awaiting the arrival of a much-wanted baby.

I got out of the Buick, then headed up the walk.

"What's up, girlfriend?" Tina asked. Her voice was perky, but she tried a little too hard. She looked younger than her early thirties, cute in her white cut-off jeans and floral cami, her feet bare, toes painted a sparkly pink.

"Everything okay?" Kevin chimed in. He was a handsome devil in khaki shorts and a plain white T, his somewhat unruly sandy hair lightened by the summer sun.

What hung in the air was the unspoken "... *with the baby?*"

I said, "I'm feeling great and the baby is fine," as I headed for one of the rockers to sit down. "I just wanted to share some news with you two, before it got around town."

"What is your Mother spreading *now?*" Tina asked, taking the other rocker.

Kevin stretched out on the top step, his back against the railing post, head turned toward me.

"This is one slice of gossip Mother isn't likely to serve up," I said.

"Nothing terrible, I hope," Tina said.

I took a moment to settle into the rocker. "Kind of hard to qualify it, actually. Really . . . pretty bad, I guess."

Tina's smiled faded as she sat forward. "What is it, honey?"

Suddenly I had a crushing sensation in my chest and couldn't breathe.

I started making horrible, gasping sounds, and Kevin jumped up and grabbed me as I fell onto my knees, fighting for air.

"Call 911!" he shouted to Tina.

But a self-composed Tina said, "No. This isn't the baby. Brandy's having a panic attack—she's had them before. I know what to do."

My friend knelt beside me, one arm around my shoulders, and as I continued to gasp, she commanded, "Breathe slower . . . not so fast . . . that's right . . . slower still . . . now deeper." Then, soothingly, "You're not going to die, sweetie . . . you'll be all right . . . nothing's going to happen."

As quickly as the attack came, it went, leaving me exhausted.

And frightened.

Would it happen again? And what if I was alone? Who would talk me down from the ledge? And what if I was behind the wheel of my car?

Tina helped me back into the rocker while Kevin hurried off to fetch some water.

"I'm all right," I managed.

Tina held out her arms and smiled goofily. "Will you look at my hands—I'm *shaking!*"

"Me, too."

We both started to laugh. Our laughter was relieved and had just the tiniest hint of hysteria.

Frowning, Kevin returned with a glass of water. "I didn't realize it was funny," he said with a tentative smile, handing me the drink. He looked a little shook up himself.

I took a sip, then said, "Haven't had one of *those* for a long time. The Prozac must have kept 'em at bay."

Tina settled at my feet, crossing her legs, Indian-style. "Maybe you should go back on the Prozac," she suggested gently.

I shook my head. "I don't want anything to hurt your baby."

Kevin, having settled back on the porch step, said softly, "Maybe it would be *best* for the baby. . . ."

I waved a dismissive hand. "I had a panic attack because of this damn hot weather."

They were both looking at me suspiciously.

"And, well . . . there could be *another* reason. I suppose it could be because of what I came here to tell you."

Tina and Kevin waited patiently, their eyes clouded with concern, while I collected my thoughts.

"About nine months ago," I began, "I received an anonymous letter in the mail. . . ."

I went over the poison-pen soap opera of the past six months, including the content of the letters right down to my parentage, and ending with that morning's episode—Mother's scuffle with Connie in the clock shop.

My friends looked stunned.

Teen said, "I can hardly believe it! All this time, and Peggy Sue never *told* you?"

"And what about *Senator Clark?*" Kevin put in, spitting

the name out like it was something foul. "You can't tell me he didn't know—and here I *voted* for that bum!"

I let them go on for a while, watching their shock turn to indignation and then came the inevitable hurt from Tina.

"Brandy," my best friend asked plaintively, "why didn't you tell me sooner? Why didn't you trust me with this? You must have been suffering."

It was a valid question; we never kept *anything* from each other.

I locked eyes with her. "I don't know, Teen. I guess I just hoped the whole thing would go away like a bad dream." I gave her a chagrined smirk. "Anyway, I didn't suffer that much—remember, I was on Prozac through most of it."

Tina nodded, her expression forgiving. "I understand. Coming here tonight? That *had* to be difficult."

Kevin asked, "Who all knows about this?"

"Peggy Sue, Mother, Senator Clark I'm pretty sure, and now you two. . . . And the instigator, of course—Connie Grimes herself. Wicked Witch of the . . . which one had the house fall on her again?"

Teen touched my knee. "You're *sure* the letters came from her?"

I nodded. "She as much as admitted it."

Kevin looked out across the lawn, where darkness had crept in. "There must be a way to stop her."

I slapped at a mosquito. "I don't think there is one— that woman is hell-bent for leather to ruin us."

Tina was getting to her feet. "What does that mean, anyway . . . 'hell-bent for leather'?"

I stood with a sigh. "Don't know . . . but it fits her to a T." Another expression I didn't understand. "I should go."

Kevin rose, kissed me on the cheek, then retreated inside, giving us girls some privacy.

"Why don't you let me drive you home?" Tina asked as we made our way down the porch steps. "Kev can follow in his car."

"No, honey. I'll be fine. Honestly."

Our conversation was accompanied by a chorus of cicadas and crickets.

Tina said, "Brandy, I *am* worried about you having another panic attack. Won't you please consider going back on—"

"Look, we've been over that. Nothing but aspirin." We were at my car now. "But I will go see my therapist, and talk to her about this latest attack."

"Promise?"

I smiled. "Girl Scout's honor."

She gave me a hug, then held me by my forearms, her eyes painfully earnest. "You know there isn't *anything* I wouldn't do for you. Kevin, too. We both love you."

I touched her cheek. "I know. Please don't worry. As somebody much smarter than me once said, 'This too shall pass.' " I opened the car door. "And after all, I'm not the real victim in this—it's Peggy Sue and Mother who will have to face what's to come."

Tina shuddered. "And your sister so values the opinions of others."

"Tell me about it. And Mother hates being on the wrong end of gossip. . . ."

That got a little laugh out of Teen, and I got in my car, backed out of the drive. I watched her in my rearview mirror, still standing in the driveway, smaller and smaller until the darkness swallowed her.

What *was* to come?

Mother ridiculed.

Sis ostracized.

And me caught in the middle.

*   *   *

The next morning I slept in later than usual, and when I finally made it downstairs there was a note from Mother taped to the coffee machine (I would not give *that* up for *any* baby) saying she had taken the gas-driven trolley downtown to do some personal business (i.e., snooping).

This gave me the privacy I needed to get Connie Grimes on the phone. The conversation was fairly brief.

"I'd like to come and talk to you," I said.

"Talk to my lawyer. Violate that restraining order at your own risk."

"I'll only stop by if you give me permission."

"Why should I? I can tell you right now what my plans are—I'm going to have your mother arrested, and that little dog of yours put down. For attacking me."

Getting Mother arrested was one thing, but threatening to have Sushi put to sleep? I felt my face flush and I had to tell myself this was just Connie blustering—after all, a day had passed, and neither the police nor animal control had shown up at our door. . . .

So I took a deep breath, let it out, and replaced my fear and anger with a gently ribbing tone.

"Ah, come on, Con—imagine the fun you'll have . . . me, groveling at your feet? You really want your attorney to be the one who hears me beg for mercy?"

Long pause. "All right. Come at noon. . . . I'll be at bridge club until then."

After tending to Sushi—breakfast followed by a shot of insulin and the obligatory payoff of a treat—I decided to forgo my shower, and put on a pair of sloppy maternity shorts and an oversized gray T-shirt. Figured I might as well look *really* pathetic, as I pleaded with Connie to undeclare her war against us.

By now Soosh had figured out I was heading somewhere, and was dancing at my feet, unaware that Connie Grimes wanted to see her take a very long doggie nap.

So I scooped her up, saying, "You have an apology to make, girl, and are going to be on your bestest, and cutest, behavior!"

She cocked her head in "huh" fashion, but willingly allowed herself to be stuffed into my front carry-on.

Full disclosure: I entertained only the slightest hope of Connie backing off. What seemed more likely was that my hostess would verbally reveal herself in all her vengeful glory . . .

. . . in which case, I would capture her misbehavior on a small tape recorder hidden in a pocket of my spacious shorts.

The Borne girls weren't the only ones in Serenity who could have their reputations ruined.

Would you think less of me (or is that *even* less?) if I were to type the following: *Heh heh heh.* . . .

At eleven-thirty, under a sunny sky for such dark skulduggery, I headed out to my Buick. For the ride over, I had move Sushi from my baby pouch to the rider's seat, where she stood at the window and, paws just reaching the glass, stared out fascinated at a world gliding by that she could probably only discern as the vaguest blur.

This was a little early to be leaving for my noon appointment, but I thought Sushi and I would sit in Connie's drive and devise our strategy—come up with things I could say that would *really* set my reluctant hostess off. (I was not counting on much strategic input from Soosh.)

The witch (with a *b*) lived across town in a subdivision designated Hidden Pines, despite the developer having chopped down all the pine trees to make way for the houses. Those pines were *really* hidden. For much of the 1980s, Hidden Pines had been *the* place to live for the well-heeled of Serenity; but time marches on, and so do subdivisions, one new one coming after the other, each making the former seem less fashionable.

Not that HP wasn't still nice. But it was filled with split-level homes that had long since gone out of style, and with good reason: who wants to walk up a bunch of steps to their house, then be confronted with more steps inside? Especially if you're loaded down with groceries.

Connie's home was at the end of a cul-de-sac, white with gray shutters and a green-tiled roof. The manicured lawn was tastefully studded with fruit trees and a couple of colorful flower beds. But a stone bubbling fountain to one side of the front entrance seemed too grand for the mid-price-range home, a tip-off to Connie's higher aspirations.

I frankly didn't know much about the woman's family. Just that Connie's husband, Fred, worked at a luxury car dealership, and that her two married boys lived at opposite ends of the country, as far away from her as they could get, without falling in an ocean.

We were sitting in the car only a few minutes before it became too hot for a pregnant woman and a blind dog to remain there, even with the windows powered down, so I got out. Anyway, Sushi aside, you're not supposed to leave a baby in a closed car, and a baby inside of me inside a closed car qualified.

An unclaimed package on the front porch meant Connie wasn't home yet, so I walked around the side of the house, hoping to find a back patio where I could park myself—preferably in the nice cool shade of a tree. I let Sushi down—she would not stray far from me in this foreign land, not without bumping her little noggin, anyway.

On hand was a large cement area with mismatched patio furniture, overcrowded planters, clinking wind chimes, and whirling miniature windmills—all being watched over by hordes of ceramic gnomes.

So this wonderland of questionable taste was the *real* Connie Grimes.

Still, Sushi somehow navigated her way to a sliding patio door that stood slightly ajar. She stuck her little head inside, the rest of her not able to squeeze through, her bushy little tail twitching at me.

What the heck. I went over and slid the door open just enough to give Sushi a little more relief from the heat.

But before I could even say, *"Stay,"* she dashed inside. Instead, *I* stayed—framed in the doorway—heat on my back, air-conditioning on my front, an oddly pleasant sensation—then finally followed Sushi in.

I couldn't even be mad at her.

Hadn't Mother always said that an unlocked door was an open invitation? And who were Sushi and I to doubt her wisdom? (Those are rhetorical questions. No answering required.)

I stepped into the kitchen, which opened onto an entertainment room at my left—comfy couch and recliner, smallish flat-screen TV, and brick fireplace. Sushi had deposited herself on the kitchen's cool tile floor, her legs spread out like a collapsed card table, her little face ecstatic with the coolness of the flooring on her tummy.

"Guess I don't have to tell you to stay," I said.

The kitchen was tiny by current standards, but had nice appliances, and was clean and neat. Some of the kitsch on the patio, however, had crept inside, like mold—starting with the collection of small frogs arranged on the sill of the sink window, and a display of Elvis plates on one wall.

Still, there was something familiar about the rooms, and then it came to me: they were similar to Peggy Sue's—color schemes, furnishings, even wallpaper. Except this was a less expensive version, on a smaller scale.

Good grief, I thought, and why I was suddenly talking like a *Peanuts* character I couldn't tell you. But . . . was Connie obsessed with my sister? If so, why would she want to destroy the object of her obsession?

I sat on a bar stool at the kitchen counter to wait like a good girl for my hostess. But after a moment, I got bored—*and* hungry (preggers gals do that)—and slid off. Soon I was poking my head in the fridge.

And here's where, admittedly, I may have, yes, crossed the line—I made myself a turkey sandwich, then washed it down with a glass of milk.

Followed by a couple of Twinkies.

Of course, Sushi was off the tile floor and dancing at my feet throughout, the lure of food trumping cool comfort. I slipped her some of the turkey, but said, through a mouthful of Twinkie, "Not good for dogs!"

Like it was good for me?

Finally she slunk off.

Now noon was here and still no sign of Connie, so I continued to snoop in the kitchen. I found mismatched glasses, chipped everyday dishes, an incomplete cutlery set, and pans with flaking Teflon.

In a walk-in pantry, I discovered a laptop computer, and was about to turn it on for a look when Sushi appeared in the open doorway, whining to get my attention.

"I said, not *good* for dogs."

But that wasn't it—her whine was something different, almost a wail.

How odd.

I exited the pantry to follow Soosh, who had *(whoops!)* left a trail of muddy paw prints down the hallway.

The prints ended at the mouth of the living room, but upon closer inspection, the prints had a reddish tinge, not like mud, not even red clay.

More like blood.

Was Sushi hurt?

Alarm spiked through me, as the animal had disappeared into the living room. Any concern of the mess she might make (beyond those bloody paws, she was house-

broken) (sort of) was blotted out by her continued whining, which was working itself into a little shih tzu howl.

Then I spotted the doggie's tail making like a windshield
wiper, between the floral couch and glass coffee table.

"Here, Soosh, here, Soosh," I said, moving forward.
"Are you okay, baby?"

Then a bare foot—not a paw, a human foot—came into
view, followed by a blue dress, and I found Sushi, staring
sightlessly into the equally sightless eyes of Connie
Grimes.

Who looked upset.

You would be, too, with a knife in your chest.

A Trash 'n' Treasures Tip

Before spending a substantial amount on an antique,
make sure you have a money-back guarantee of its au-
thenticity. A reputable dealer should be willing to comply.
Otherwise, bye-bye buy.

Chapter Three

Knock-worst

I waited on the stoop of Connie's split-level home for the paramedics to arrive. After calling 911, I had washed off Sushi's bloody little paws in the sink, wondering if I was destroying evidence or something, then tied her up with her leash to a well-shaded wrought-iron patio table, providing her with a dish of water. Tampering with a crime scene? I was in so deep, it could hardly matter.

Finally the ambulance arrived, with no siren. No need. A Mutt and Jeff team emerged, one man tall and slender, the other short and stocky (reverse that: isn't Mutt the little one?).

"The dead woman's in the living room," I told them. "And it's a crime scene, so please take whatever precautions you need to."

They both gave me a funny look, clearly taken aback, receiving policelike instructions from a pregnant woman in a gray T-shirt and sloppy shorts.

Maybe it sounded funny to them. But the last thing I needed was the area compromised any more than I already had, and make me even more the prime suspect.

But they didn't say anything, just hurried inside, and I followed, retreating to the kitchen to wait for the actual police to arrive, which would most likely be two uniformed officers in the closest patrol car. Unfortunately, thanks to Mother's penchant for involving herself in murder cases, I was becoming an old hand at this.

So I was a little surprised when the chief himself walked into the kitchen.

Chief Tony Cassato, that is.

Serenity's top cop, a man of mystery whose background was the source of many rumors (any number generated by Mother) and whose big-city no-nonsense demeanor made him one of the most respected, if controversial public servants around.

Also my current boyfriend.

Our friendship went back a few years—when I was home for a while to guide Mother through one of her mental crises, I'd helped Tony institute a new policy of handling mentally ill perps. That friendship had blossomed over the past six months and—while we were not exactly, shall we say, full-fledged lovers (due to the condition I was in)—we were certainly more than just friends.

Tony—late forties, barrel-chested, gray temples, steel-gray eyes, bulbous nose, square jaw—wore his usual summer attire of short-sleeved white shirt, gray slacks, and black Florsheims.

Those bullet-hard eyes, though laced with concern, bore into mine. "Brandy, are you all right?"

"Yes, considering." Then I whispered, "Please, don't let them louse this up—your forensics team?"

He frowned, half-concern, half-irritation. "What?"

"I *really* don't want to have this baby in jail. . . ." My voice cracked at the end.

Tony pulled up a bar stool. "Okay, let's just take it easy," he said. He managed to smile. I could tell it took some effort. "Nobody's going to louse anything up—my guys know what they're doing."

I fluttered a hand; I had a queasy feeling. Probably the Twinkies. "But I've been here at least an hour, and my fingerprints must be all over this kitchen."

I was thinking specifically about the cutlery set that I may or may not have touched—whose missing knife was lodged in Connie's chest.

Tony was working at keeping his voice gentle, calm. "Brandy, why were you here?"

"Waiting for Connie. We had a sort of appointment, to talk."

"What about that restraining order?"

"She invited me. I had her permission. Of course, I can't *prove* that now...." I put a hand to my head. "Oh, Lord ... *please* let her have been dead a while."

Tony apparently did not know what to say to that.

A uniformed cop appeared. I knew the tall and gangly Officer Munson from several murder investigations Mother and I had (let's say) helped with in the past.

If I had been Chief Cassato, about now I'd be wondering if Mother and I were serial killers who had framed all those brought to justice in the other murder cases. Weren't *we* the common denominator?

If "common" was the right word.

"The coroner's here," Officer Munson told Tony.

I touched the chief's hand, where it rested on the counter. "Do we *really* need the coroner? I mean ... you don't have to be a doctor to tell the woman's dead. And that's just one more person to tromp through this crime scene and—"

"Will you let me do my job?" Tony cut in, not unkindly.

Munson was giving me a look as if I were half out of my mind, which was most uncalled for.

Tony told the young officer, "Tell Bert to examine the body later, at the hospital." The morgue was in the basement. Of the hospital, not Connie's house.

Munson nodded and scooted.

The chief's attention was back on me. "Brandy, let's go over it. Nice and calm. Step at a time. Now—what are you doing here?"

He had already dug in a pocket of his slacks and withdrawn a pen and small notepad—which I liked, because it was not nearly as intimidating as a tape recorder.

Still, a little too defensively, I answered, "I told you I had an appointment. I was invited."

"Okay . . . but *why*? You weren't exactly friends with the woman."

He was referring to that public row I'd had with Connie last year, requiring me to take an anger management course. And inspiring that damned, damning restraining order.

Choosing my words carefully, I told him what had happened yesterday morning at the clock repair shop. But not *why* it happened. And I left out Sushi ripping Connie's dress. No need to make a suspect out of Soosh.

"What did the Grimes woman say," Tony asked, "that made your mother attack her?"

"Mother didn't attack Connie, exactly."

"What did Vivian do, exactly?"

"She . . . gave Connie a little push."

"A little push?"

"A push."

"Okay, a push. Now back to my question—*why* did she give the Grimes woman a push?"

The answer was tricky. What could I say that was the truth, if not quite the whole truth? Something that wouldn't contradict what Mr. Timmons might say?

I pretended to be working to summon up the precise words and finally came out with, "Connie said something like, 'Well, if it isn't mother and daughter.' "

When I didn't continue, a frowning Tony asked, "That's *it? That* caused your mother to shove her?"

I shrugged. "I was busy with Mr. Timmons, showing him our clock. Besides, it wasn't *what* Connie said so much as *how* she said it. Her tone was all nasty, and her face was all screwed up." I stopped, then added, "I don't know *why* that woman hates us so much . . . *hated* us so much. . . ."

I was fishing for a little sympathy, but I didn't get a nibble.

Tony sighed. Weight of the world. "All right, Brandy. So you came here at Connie's invitation. To do what? Make amends?"

"That's it," I said, perhaps too eagerly. "Make amends."

"And?"

I shrugged. "And she wasn't home yet, and it was hot outside, and the patio door was open. Sushi nosed her way in, to get into the air-conditioning, and I just . . . followed. I figured Connie left the door open for me. So it wasn't breaking and entering or trespassing or anything."

"I didn't imply it was, Brandy."

Officer Munson reappeared. "Chief! I can't locate the husband—Fred Grimes? Apparently he's still at lunch, and his cell phone is going to voice mail. I suppose we could wait till he contacts us."

"I *suppose,*" Tony said as if to a small, slow child, "you could go over there and wait until he *does* show."

The officer gulped and nodded and disappeared again.

Tony turned to me. He clearly did not want to upset me, however upset *with* me he might be. "Brandy, did you go anywhere else in the house?"

"No. Just here. And the pantry."

"The pantry?"

"I, uh . . . made myself a sandwich."

Tony raised his eyebrows.

So I raised mine back at him. "I was *hungry.* I'd been here a while. I'm eating for two, you know!"

He let out some air, apparently trying to make it sound like something other than a sigh, as he scribbled in the little notebook.

I volunteered, "Then I heard Sushi whining and went to see what was wrong . . . and that's when I saw Connie."

He wrote some more.

His eyes raised to mine; they were hooded and unblinking. "Anything else you think you should mention?"

"Such as?"

"Oh, I don't know . . . maybe something you may later regret *not* mentioning."

"Well."

"Well?"

"I did eat a Twinkie."

"You ate a Twinkie?"

"All right—two Twinkies. You know, one package. You don't eat one and let the other go to waste, right? Right?"

This time he didn't disguise the sigh. He closed the notebook and it was like a tiny slap. I jumped a little.

"All right, Brandy," he said. "That's all—for now."

Cops loved to say that.

I said, "And I won't leave town."

"What?"

"Isn't that what you always tell suspects? Don't leave town?"

"Is that what you are, Brandy? A suspect?"

"You tell me."

"Okay. Don't leave town."

If there was sarcasm in that, it was very, very dry.

I slid off the stool. Tony escorted me gently by the arm down the short hallway, and past the living room, where the forensics team—two men and one woman in those plastic suits that are like full-body condoms—were still working in the room. Connie's corpse *(yikes)* had been quietly removed during my questioning.

Outside, in the warmth of the sunny day, Tony asked, "You gonna be okay driving home?"

"Sure."

"Really? Because you look terrible."

"Gee, thanks. You always know just what to say to a girl."

He rested a hand on my shoulder. "That's not what I meant and you know it. You've taken a hell of a shock and I'm worried about you."

"You are?"

"I am. I'll be glad to drive you myself if necessary."

"No, really I'm okay."

"All right, then. Go home and get some rest."

"I will. And Tony? Thank you. Thanks for . . . caring."

His smile was barely discernible, but it was there. So was his nod.

I went around back to the patio and collected Sushi, tucked her in the pouch, then on my return gave the chief a little wave.

But I could feel his unblinking steel-gray eyes on me as I walked to my car.

I dropped Sushi off at home—Mother was off on her trolley escapades—and went into the kitchen and splashed water on my face. I don't remember deciding to go over to Peggy Sue's—in fact I barely recall driving over there—but somehow I arrived unscathed, pulling up to an open garage, where Sis was unloading groceries from the hatchback of her powder-blue Cadillac Escalade.

She looked almost pleased to see me.

"Oh, good," she said, after I'd vacated my Buick (no

engine knocking or passing wind this time). "You can help me."

That was Sis, all right—always ready to ask a pregnant woman to carry heavy sacks for her.

Peggy Sue shopped at the nicest, most expansively stocked store in town—HyVee—while Mother and I checked and bagged our own groceries at the discount place, where items were generic and not even removed from the packing cartons.

I selected a couple of light-looking sacks and followed Sis through a garage door that led directly into the kitchen.

When we'd both set our bags on a counter, I said, "I take it you haven't heard about Connie."

"What about her?" Sis asked, beginning to unload a sack. I waited until she had put a jar of Ragu (Zesty) down on the counter. No need for another mess.

"You better brace yourself, Peg.... Connie is... dead."

I managed not to precede "dead" with "ding dong the witch is." Even I wasn't that cruel. But I did think it.

Peggy Sue froze, one hand poised over a sack as if she were trying to unload it via telekinesis. "*What?*"

I nodded, reaching in and taking the next jar from her sack. "Connie is gone. Deceased."

Suddenly I was doing the Monty Python Dead Parrot routine.

"When?" she asked. "How? *What . . . ?*"

"I said brace yourself—somebody killed her. This morning."

"Killed her?"

"Yeah. She was murdered." My laugh had no humor in it. "Funny. Connie Grimes was somebody I often wished dead, in that casual way you say such things about people you dislike. Or let's face it, hate. But it was awful, Peg.

Somebody stabbed her. Right in the chest. The heart. I took absolutely no satisfaction in finding her like that."

"Well, I should hope not! Wait, what . . . ? You *found* her?"

I nodded. "Yup. I would imagine I'm looking like the primest of prime suspects. If the chief weren't my boyfriend, I'd probably have been booked by now."

Sis leaned back against the counter. "Oh, dear Lord. . . . Tell me everything. Everything you did, everything you know."

I gave her the full rundown, from this morning on—setting the noon appointment, driving over there, wandering inside, eating Twinkies, hearing the whining Sushi that drew me to the body. Sounded like one of the Perry Mason novels Mother's Red-Hatted League book club was reading: *The Case of the Whining Dog.*

"So *that's* why Connie was a no-show at bridge club this morning," Peggy Sue was saying. Her shock had ebbed. "I was actually going to talk to her today myself."

"So, then, uh . . . *you* didn't kill her?"

"*Brandy!* How could you even *think* such a thing?"

I shrugged. "Considering what we talked about yesterday when I was over here, it seems like a perfectly reasonable question."

Sis arched one perfectly shaped eyebrow. "What about *you*, Brandy?"

"Like I said—I thought about it. Just a sick fantasy. Running more to sticking a voodoo pin in a Connie doll and having her pass away in her sleep. Never dreamed the pin would be a knife."

I shuddered. So did Sis.

"You and Mother," she said, and shivered.

"What *about* me and Mother?"

"You two . . . you *attract* this kind of thing."

"No. Absolutely not. We do not attract it. Even Mother

doesn't attract it. Now, she does go *looking* for it . . . that I'll give you."

Peg's expression was glazed. "And what *about* Mother? Where was *she* this morning?"

"Downtown. On the trolley, then off it. You know—her usual haunts."

My sister sighed. "Well, that's a relief, anyway . . . especially since she's been so fruity lately."

I shook my head. "I've done everything to get her back on her meds short of tying her to a chair and using a funnel."

Sis, returning to unloading the sack, sighed heavily. "What a horrible thing."

"Using a funnel on Mother?"

"Connie getting killed!"

"Is it really?"

She stopped and stared at me.

"Oh, don't look so shocked. I didn't really wish her dead, and if I could will her back to life, I would . . . though I'd hate myself in the morning. Face it, Sis—somebody did us a favor. Secret contained?"

"Well . . . it's awful to look at it that way, but I guess . . . I guess you do have a point."

We fell silent for a few long moments. Guilt, regret, even sorrow draped the kitchen. But so did relief.

Finally Sis said, strangely chipper, "You know, Brandy, I bet Connie's death doesn't have anything to do with us. Not a thing."

"She probably did have her share of enemies," I admitted. "If she was writing *us* poisoned pen letters, she could have been doing the same with all other sorts of folks around Serenity."

"Yes!" Sis said, latching on to that eagerly, adding, "And there have been quite a few break-ins around town lately, what with the bad economy."

I nodded. "You got that right—especially during the mornings and afternoons, when working couples are gone, their kids in day care or school."

Peggy Sue's eyes flared. "That's *surely* what happened! A burglar broke into Connie's house, not expecting anyone to be home, and then panicked when he saw her."

I was into it. "And Connie came at him with the knife, and he turned the tables on her!"

"Sure! That sounds just like her. For whatever her faults, she had spine. Spunk." Sis rubbed my upper arm. "Sweetheart, I think everything's going to be all right, don't you?"

Hearing her call me "sweetheart" gave me a surprising rush of warmth. "Me, too. Me, too."

Of course, if Peggy Sue really thought that, she wasn't near as smart as I thought she was.

And if I believed that, I was even dumber than I thought I was.

Arriving home in the late afternoon, I found Mother in the kitchen, baking up a storm.

"What's going on?" I asked.

Because lately, a home-cooked meal was a rarity around the Borne household, and in progress was a feast for a small army: twin pans of lasagna, pot roast, chili, and a casserole I couldn't identify.

(If you look up the word *casserole* in the dictionary it says, "An unidentifiable food dish.")

Mother gestured to a stack of plastic storage containers with a wooden spoon dripping something or other. "I'm freezing meals!"

"Freezing meals. Okay." That funnel idea was looking ever more rational. "Why are you freezing meals, Mother?"

"Why, for you to have *later,* dear."

Not "us," but me. Was she anticipating her inevitable

mental nosedive? She had only been institutionalized a handful of times, but the possibility was always there.

"Did you hear about Connie?" I asked.

Silly question—I could hear the staticky crackling of the police scanner that held its exalted place atop the refrigerator.

Mother wiped her hands on the red-checkered apron she always wore when cooking. "Oh, *my*, yes! Stabbed to death. *Exciting* news, isn't it?"

And I thought *I'd* been cruel. "Gee, Mother, that's . . . that's pretty harsh."

Mother frowned. "Yes, you're right. Shame on me. Everybody has *some* good in them. Even a blankety-blank like the late Connie Grimes." (In case you're wondering, she actually said "blankety-blank.")

So she'd heard.

I asked, "But did you know *I* was the one who found Connie?"

Mother nearly dropped her pan of lasagna.

"What?" If her eyes had grown any larger, they would have overflowed her thick lenses. "Good heavens! What were *you* doing there?"

I told her about making the appointment.

"*When* were you there?"

I told her that, too. Twinkies and all.

"You're not a suspect, are you, dear?"

I shrugged. "Probably. A 'person of interest,' at least."

Mother suddenly looked ashen; she sat down on the red fifties-era kitchen stepladder stool that would have been worth a pretty penny if we hadn't used it so hard.

"Oh, this *is* unfortunate," she moaned, one hand theatrically pressed to her forehead, palm out. "One might say tragic!"

"Murders generally are." But for all her melodrama, I was sorry that I'd alarmed her, and said, "Hey, I'm sure the police will clear me."

Mother nodded. "Yes . . . yes. After all, they aren't *completely* incompetent."

I wouldn't tell Tony she said that.

"I'd imagine the time of death *alone* would clear you," Mother was saying. "Why, I'm as sure of that as what day it is." She frowned. "What day *is* it, dear?"

"Well . . ." I gave it some thought. "Wednesday."

She looked at me earnestly. "You do know the garbage *must* go out tonight."

"Yes, Mother." I'd been putting it out ever since I'd moved home. Why would she ask that? Funnel anyone?

She stood from the stool with a beaming sigh. "Good. *Now.* Where are those papers I need you to sign?"

"What papers?"

Not replying, Mother went into the dining room, and I followed in confusion; she pulled out a chair at the table, gesturing for me to do the same.

"This is a Power of Attorney over my finances, giving you full control," Mother said, tapping a legal document with a forefinger.

So she did figure it had come time for her to be institutionalized; and she wasn't fighting it.

"Is signing this really necessary? I've always been able to handle things before. . . ."

She sighed and her eyes rose upward as if heaven were calling. "I'm afraid I might be away for some time, dear."

This was the most candid Mother had ever been with me regarding her "condition"—as she referred to it—and also the most foresight she'd ever shown. On some level, it seemed to me, this was progress. She was not only willing to go away for treatment, she was preparing for her absence in a well-organized, logical fashion. This was not just a good sign, but the end of an era, and the dawning of a new age of acceptance of her mental problems.

So I dutifully signed the papers.

"*That's* a good girl," she said. "Are you hungry?"

I'd come home famished, but the collective smells of the lasagna, chili, pot roast, and mystery casserole wafting from the kitchen made my stomach lurch.

"Actually, I'm really beat," I said. "I think I'll go up-stairs and lie down for a while."

"Good idea, dear. You can always have something to eat later."

She had a point. I made my way upstairs (no trundling!) and conked out for a good three hours, dreaming wild nonsense, which upon awaking only left me more ex-hausted than before.

Downstairs in the living room, I found notes taped everywhere: the thermostat ("keep at 72 degrees; change filter in October"); the TV ("call cable and drop the movie channels—unless you want them"); the walnut Queen Anne armchair ("use only Kramer's oil"). All in her famil-iar flowery scrawl. Similar instructions were peppered throughout the rest of the house.

Mother appeared from the kitchen, sans apron.

"Ah . . . I see you've noticed my missives," she said cheerfully.

"They're pretty hard to miss." Then I said gently, "Can we talk?"

Mother raised her eyebrows. "Why certainly, my child—where should we go?"

I motioned to the antique needlepoint couch that faced the picture window onto the world.

We sat.

"Mother," I began. "I don't want you to worry about anything while you're gone."

"Oh, I won't, dear."

"The time will pass very quickly."

"They say it does."

"Just know that I love you, and that—"

I was going to say that I'd visit her every day, but the words caught in my throat.

As I began to try again, I could see out the picture window a police car roll up to the curb.

And the chief himself got out.

"Mother!" I grabbed her hand.

"Don't be worried, dear," she said soothingly. "He's only come to tell you that you're not a suspect."

In another moment Tony was knocking, and Mother called, *"Enter stage left!"* and then the chief was coming toward us as we both rose from the couch.

Tony positioned himself before me and took my hands, looking down into my eyes. "Brandy, I'm sorry to have to do this."

Oh, dear Lord . . . I am going to have the baby in prison!

But then his eyes traveled to Mother.

"Vivian, I'm arresting you for the murder of Connie Grimes. You have the right to remain silent, you have the right to—"

"I fully understand my rights, Chief Cassato," Mother interrupted. "And I freely admit to killing that horrible woman."

I stared at her, agape.

She turned to me and beamed. "You see, dear, I *told* you everything would be all right!"

A Trash 'n' Treasures Tip

Sometimes, a disreputable dealer will disassemble an authentic antique and create several copies by mingling real with fake parts, and pass them off as 100% originals. Mother once bought a small Victorian chair whose graceful, genuine back tapered into legs stamped—too tiny for her eyesight to capture—"Made in China."

Chapter Four

Knock-kneed

At nine the next morning, with Mother's arraignment scheduled at ten, Peggy Sue and I met with our family lawyer, Wayne Cyrus Ekhardt, at his office downtown in the Laurel Building.

Mr. Ekhardt had rocketed to fame around here in the 1950s when he got a woman off for "accidentally" shooting her cheating husband in the back four times. He was a little older than the eight-story Art Deco edifice he once owned, having run a thriving law practice there for five decades before selling the property to an engineering firm, on the stipulation that he could have the top floor rent-free for life.

Whoever made that deal had probably long since been fired, because Ekhardt was now ninety with his practice still ongoing, if limited and by appointment only—pretty much us, and a handful of other longtime clients. Of course, Mother alone kept him busy.

Sis (wearing a Burberry plaid cotton shirtdress) and I (wearing the yellow Juicy Couture sundress) stepped off the elevator and into a film noir world unchanged since the Laurel Building had been erected. While the other floors had been modernized with the times, the eighth retained the old scuffed black-and-white speckled ceramic-tile flooring, scarred-wood office doors with ancient pebbled glass, Art Moderne sconce wall lighting, and even an old porcelain drinking fountain.

Mr. Ekhardt occupied the last corner office with a scenic view of the river. Usually it was Mother and I who made the long walk down the hallway to see the lawyer, with Mother trying every doorknob of the unoccupied offices, hoping to find one unlocked, and discover a roomful of abandoned furniture that had become antiques—a procedure that would continue until I would finally go (in full Jack Benny mode), "Now cut that out!" Or words to that effect.

Now *I* found myself doing the same knob-jiggling thing, and it was Peggy Sue who snapped, "Will you quit doing that please?"

"Okay," I said sheepishly.

We walked through a patch of striped crime-shadow lighting courtesy of some Venetian blinds.

"I thought Mr. Ekhardt had passed away," she said.

"Not so that you'd notice," I said. "And it's unlikely you would, since *you've* never been the daughter who accompanies Mother when she's dealing with her legal problems." Couldn't resist the dig.

"Why can't we get a *real* lawyer?"

"You mean, one who is more socially prominent?"

"Must you make me sound terrible? I simply mean an attorney who doesn't make his reputation getting criminals off."

"First of all, Mother is accused of murder—no, make that, she has *confessed* to murder. That would make her a criminal."

"Brandy, don't be ridiculous."

I stopped, and she stopped, interrupting our gunshot footsteps on the ceramic flooring. "Do *you* want to pay for the services of some hotshot attorney?" Then added, "You may find it interesting to know that Mr. Ekhardt discounts *his* services for Mother."

Actually, sometimes we never even received a bill. Whether the elderly man forgot, or was just being nice, I couldn't say. But we certainly never questioned it or reminded him.

We were walking again when Sis said, "Well, I can tell you why Mother gets special rates from Mr. Ekhardt. Actually, I'm surprised he even sends her a *reduced* bill."

"Really? Why is that?"

She shrugged and her expression was knowingly smug. "It's because he was once in love with her."

I stopped again. *"What?"*

So did Peg. "That's right. They once had . . ." And, I swear to God, she sang, ". . . a thing going on."

Actually, I wasn't surprised—well, the singing part surprised me a little; but not this juicy vintage item about Mother and our lawyer. Mother had remained a statuesque, lovely Dane, well into her sixties; after Dad had passed, she received many marriage proposals. There were probably any number of old boys who would overlook her eccentric reputation for a slice of that well-preserved Danish strudel. (I think I just made myself sick. . . .)

Anyway, Peggy Sue and I arrived at the last pebbled-glass door, where stencils applied many decades ago now read:

WAY E EK AR T
ATTO NEY AT LA

Sis gave me a look—definitely *not* her idea of a socially prominent attorney. . . .

The door was unlocked and I pushed it open, the ancient hinges squeaking long and loud, like in a haunted house in an old movie, but still not loud enough to wake the room's only inhabitant, sitting back in his chair, mouth open, eyes shut, behind an old, scarred oaken desk. He was dozing so deep, in fact, that for a few moments—Peggy Sue gave me a startled look to confirm she had the same thought—I really did think the old barrister had finally passed away.

Then he snorted and his chest rose and my sister and I exchanged relieved glances.

Mr. Ekhardt, in a light blue seersucker suit and white shirt appropriate for summer around the turn of the century (century before last I mean), sat slumped, his nearly bald, liver-spotted head bowed. He seemed to all but disappear into the clothing—like a small boy who had tried on his father's suit.

Peggy Sue gave me a disgusted smirk. She whispered, "Are you *trying* to send Mother to the electric chair?"

"We don't have the death penalty in Iowa," I whispered back defensively. "Anyway, if they repealed that, it would probably be by lethal injection."

"That's comforting," Sis said, with an eyeball roll.

Ignoring that, I reached back and rapped on the glass of the door, keeping it up until Mr. Ekhardt woke up with another, more decisive snort. He drew himself up into the suit, like the Invisible Man getting dressed, then blinked his rheumy eyes several times. His smile told me he'd accomplished focusing them.

"Ah . . . little Brandy. You're here. And who's this lovely young thing?"

I approached the desk, Sis trailing reluctantly.

"This is my sister, Peggy Sue."

"Yes . . . yes! Certainly. Vivian's eldest." He gestured with a bony hand to the two old oak chairs in front. "Please, have a seat."

Once we were settled, I asked, "Have you seen Mother?"

He nodded.

"And?" I prodded.

His weary sigh began at his feet. "I'm afraid she's determined to plead guilty."

At past arraignments, no matter what the circumstances, Mother had always said, "Nolo contendere," just to be difficult.

"Is there anything you can do about that?" I asked. "I mean, Mother pleading guilty to a traffic violation is one thing, but—"

"I don't understand how the police got to her so fast," Peggy Sue interrupted, obviously on a different wavelength.

I stared at her.

"Well?" she said, glaring at me. "How did they know it was her?"

"I told you," I said patiently, "Mother's prints were on the knife handle. And Mother has been fingerprinted before. Plenty of times."

"Why," Peggy said rather grandly, "would *our* mother be fingerprinted?"

"Hello? Remember her stay in the county jail when she tried to stop the demolition of the old Uptown Theater?"

"Fine!" Sis snapped. "Even so, how could the police *positively* identify the prints as hers in a few short hours? Doesn't print identification analysis take a while? I'm just saying, maybe someone jumped to a conclusion just because Mother had that little incident with Connie at the clock repair shop. And perhaps because Mother does have a certain . . . reputation for eccentricity."

My eyebrows were doing their best to climb up off my forehead. "You think?"

Mr. Ekhardt interceded. "Your comments and questions are valid, Peggy Sue. . . ."

Sis shot me a *"See?"* look.

". . . but the reason your mother was charged so quickly is because Chief Cassato was a fingerprint identification expert with New Jersey law enforcement before he came to Serenity."

"Oh!" Sis said, like a car coming to an abrupt stop. "Well, then, I guess that's understandable. . . ."

That information I only recently learned from the chief himself, during one of our "date" evenings at his remote cabin hideaway. Also, that his expertise and testimony had been crucial in solving several big-city, mob-related killings.

But I felt we were getting sidetracked, and said, "Can we please get back to the arraignment? In less than an hour? What can be done about Mother pleading guilty?"

Ekhardt leaned forward with his elbows on the desk and tented his bony hands. He might have been praying. Seeing your mother's attorney praying is not the most encouraging sight.

Then he said, "I'm afraid . . . please, Brandy, Peggy Sue, understand the gravity of this situation . . . but my only option is to bring up Vivian's mental illness."

Sis looked horrified. "But then . . . everyone in town will *know!*"

If I'd been drinking, I would have performed a world's record spit-take. I said to her, "You mean there's somebody in Serenity who *doesn't* know?"

Mr. Ekhardt patted the air with his hands, calming us, or trying to. "Now, ladies, please . . . we really haven't much time. I can assure you I will handle this with as much discretion as possible." He turned his somber visage my way. "How long has Vivian been off her medication?"

"About three months," I said.

He nodded in thought. "Good. Good."

Sis was frowning. "What's good about it?"

The attorney said, "It paves the way for me to make a case with the judge that your mother is not currently able to make decisions for herself . . . at least not decisions that are in her own best interest. Is that all right with you?"

"Yes," I said.

Peggy Sue sat frozen.

"Sis? How's this for a headline—'MOTHER OF PEGGY SUE HASTINGS FOUND GUILTY OF MURDER'?"

Finally, she gave a reluctant nod.

Ekhardt stood from his desk, using it for support, the elderly gent seeming exhausted after our mildly confrontational consultation.

"Why don't you both run along to the courthouse," he said. "I'll be there in about ten minutes."

I was thinking that if he was going to make it over there in ten minutes, he'd better get started. But I said nothing.

Sis and I were silent as we walked back down the long corridor, passing through more film noir stripes.

At the elevator, looking rather stricken, she said, "Brandy, I . . . I'm sorry, but I don't think I can go with you to the arraignment."

"That's okay." No stomach for it.

"It would be just too . . . too . . ."

She should have let it go when I said okay. I blurted, "Embarrassing? Humiliating? A three-ring circus with Mother the demented ringmaster?"

Her smile was sickly. "I might not have put it just that way but . . . yes."

The air went out of my irritation. "That's all right, Sis . . . I do understand."

She sighed with relief. She swallowed very hard, and maybe she was tearing up.

The elevator arrived and we stepped on.

And me? Why, I wouldn't trade one of Mother's court appearances for a DVD boxed set of *Perry Mason* episodes.

Arraignments were held in a secondary courtroom on the second floor of the Serenity courthouse, a late nineteenth-century edifice of Grecian grandeur that the numbskulls (as Mother so delicately referred to them) who worked there kept trying to get torn down to make way for a new building with more space and central air-conditioning. So far Mother has been able to thwart such architectural genocide.

(I make a point of never taking Mother along when going to the courthouse for Sushi's dog license or to take care of property taxes or deal with license plate renewal . . . especially not in the summer. Some of those sweat-soaked clerks can be spiteful.)

In the mornings, the smaller courtroom was used for traffic court, when herds of ensnared citizens were processed in a quick, noisy cattle call to vehicular justice. I'd been to several of these sessions, Mother having racked up various traffic violations over the past few years. (As of now, Mother will not be eligible to drive again until she's one hundred and nine; but since she might now go to jail for the rest of her life, reclaiming her driver's license became something of a moot point.)

In the afternoons, however, this same courtroom was used for felony arraignments, with the atmosphere strikingly different: quiet, somber, and decidedly depressing, due in part to the loss of morning sunlight. I'd only attended one felony arraignment for Mother—I'd been married to Roger at the time, and came back from Chicago because the diva had chained herself to a wrecking ball that was about to demolish the old red brick YWCA building downtown. That resulted in a misdemeanor after a plea bargain; Mother served sixty days, and the YWCA became a parking lot.

Not every story has a happy ending.

The courtroom gallery consisted of two sections of benches separated by a center aisle in bride's-family, groom's-family fashion. I sat in the front row, facing the judge, to be nearer Mother, when she would appear.

It was five minutes to ten and only a handful of people were present: a middle-aged female court reporter at her machine; a young male journalist from the Serenity newspaper; a male student from the community college (I deduced this from his SCC T-shirt); and nosy Mrs. Mackelrath, who (according to Mother) attended all arraignments because of her "interest in community affairs, dear." In other words, she had nothing better to do.

A word about court reporters: think twice before going into the profession, as some states have replaced humans with a computer system called DART. But not our state—when Mother heard about the possible transition, she sprang into action, tirelessly collecting data that the new technology was too expensive, and not as reliable as the high quality of the personal touch. This research she systematically forwarded to various powers-that-be.

Her favorite *Perry Mason* episodes (yes, we do value those previously mentioned DVD boxed sets highly) are the ones where the judge says to the court reporter—usually a squirrely-looking gent with a twitchy mustache (the court reporter, not the judge)—"Read that testimony back." I don't know why Mother likes those moments the best—I prefer it when Perry leans over and tells Paul Drake to go off and do something absurd ("Paul, hire a helicopter and fly over the Grand Canyon") that will eventually crack the case.

Anyway, at two minutes to ten, the lawyers arrived, Mr. Ekhardt taking a seat on the aisle-end of my pew, and the county attorney—bespectacled, salt-and-pepper hair, nondescript navy suit—positioning himself directly across from Ekhardt. (No separate tables for Perry Mason and Hamilton Burger here.)

At precisely ten, a side door next to the judge's bench swung open and His Honor swept in, long black robe flapping like Batman's cape. The judge was pushing sixty, and pushing it hard, with silver hair and heavy bags beneath his eyes. He took his regal place behind the raised bench.

The side door opened again and a burly male bailiff in a tan uniform marched into the room, an army of one, taking a rigid position next to the flag of the USA on its sturdy if squat pole.

The only noise came from a small window air conditioner, doing its best to cool the already warm room. This hum was soon accompanied by the rustling of papers, as the judge readied for Mother's case.

I felt sick to my stomach, and was glad I'd had the foresight to skip breakfast. Whether it was pregnancy or concern for Mother, or a combo of both, I couldn't tell you.

The stern-faced judge caught the eye of the bailiff, and nodded, and the bailiff stepped back to the side door and opened it. I could see Mother waiting beyond in the custody of a female guard in a tan shirt and slacks, Mother wearing the same clothes she'd been hauled off in. The guard escorted Mother into the chamber, depositing her next to the standing bailiff, before fading back against the near wall.

Usually I took a perverse enjoyment in Mother's tilts with legal officialdom, but I suddenly sided with my sister in thinking it might be better to be anywhere else. A murder arraignment was something new and different in the Adventures of Vivian Borne, and quite disturbing. . . .

Still, Mother looked surprisingly well, her clothes not at all rumpled, silver-white hair combed neatly back into a chignon at the nape of her neck. She even wore a little lipstick.

Mother bestowed me a serene smile, and I smiled weakly back.

I crossed my fingers that she was about to put on one heck of an eccentric show—not for its entertainment value, no; rather, to play unwittingly into our lawyer's strategy.

The judge banged his gavel and everyone jumped a little in their seats. But Mother hadn't stirred. She remained serenely, spookily immobile.

"The State versus Vivian Borne," His Honor said in a properly booming voice. "Does the defendant have representation?"

"Yes, Your Honor," Ekhardt spoke up.

"For the record," the judge noted, "Wayne Ekhardt is representing the defendant."

The court reporter's fingers clicked faintly away at her machine. It sounded like little tiny tap dancers, whom I could picture in my mind. Maybe *I* should have gone for an insanity plea. . . .

The judge addressed Mother. "Mrs. Borne, do you understand the process of this arraignment?"

Mother smiled sweetly. "Oh my, yes, Your Honor. I've been through it enough times."

The judge grunted, "Very well. You are charged with felony murder. How do you plead?"

I held my breath. This is where I expected the antics to begin, with Mother rambling on incoherently until the exasperated judge would bang his gavel—if we were *really* lucky, he would bang it down on his thumb, like the last judge.

But Mother said simply, "Guilty, Your Honor. Guilty as charged."

And no more.

I looked woefully toward Mr. Ekhardt.

He rose and said, "Your Honor, permission to approach the bench?"

The district attorney seemed startled by his opponent's request, and when the judge nodded his approval, the DA followed Ekhardt up there, having to work to catch up with the old boy, in several senses.

What followed was a hushed conversation between Ekhardt, the judge, and the DA.

I could not hear what Mr. Ekhardt, or the DA, were saying, because they were facing away from me, but I did catch the occasional words from the judge, including "not established," and "unverified."

Which did not sound like good news, because he was apparently questioning Mr. Ekhardt's tactic of an insanity plea.

Mother was also straining to hear, frowning, her eyes narrow behind the large lenses, serving to make them appear normal size. *Also* not helpful.

The defendant must have been aware that her mental health was being discussed, because she said loudly, "Permission to speak, Your Honor!"

The conversation at the bench halted as the three men looked toward her. And before His Honor could respond, Mother took the spotlight, and with considerable dignity.

"This is *my* arraignment—*my* life. I am in complete control of my faculties. I understand my rights, and I plead guilty. I will not waste the court's time, the taxpayer's money, nor my own limited resources in pleading otherwise to a crime for which I take full responsibility. Nor will I put my family through the ordeal of a criminal trial."

Finally some melodrama entered in, as Mother raised a finger.

"Furthermore," she said, some ham coming in, "I cite the case of Frendak versus the United States . . . an insanity defense cannot be imposed upon an unwilling defendant if an intelligent defendant voluntarily wishes to forgo the defense—which I *do*." Then as an aside she turned to the gallery and with her eyes big and buggy, and her smile cheerfully demented, added, "I'd like to thank the fine folks at Wikipedia for that information!"

Except for that last lapse, I could not remember seeing Mother more in control of herself, or hearing her speak more lucidly.

Which made my heart sink.

The judge said solemnly, "Mrs. Borne, please understand that I have a responsibility to make sure that you are completely aware of what you are doing, and the repercussions thereof."

Mother pulled herself up even straighter. "Your Honor, I do indeed understand the letter of the law for felony murder. Class A—life without parole, unless pardoned by the governor—which is highly unlikely because I campaigned *against* that nincompoop. Class B—a maximum of twenty-five years. Class C—ten years with a fine up to ten thousand dollars. And Class D—five years and a fine up to seven thousand five hundred dollars. However, I do not qualify for either C or D, as my actions were premeditated."

The judge stared at Mother for a moment, seeming to work hard not to let his jaw drop, then sighed. "Very well, Mrs. Borne—I must pay you the respect of assuming that you know what you're doing. . . . This court accepts the plea of guilty, and Vivian Borne will be confined in the county jail until sentencing."

He banged the gavel.

It was over.

And I burst into tears.

While I bawled like a baby, the bailiff was escorting Mother through the side door. She called back to me, "Don't worry, dear! It's for the best!"

The courtroom emptied out, leaving a defeated Mr. Ekhardt seated next to a stricken me.

"Well, Brandy," he sighed wearily. "It's not the first time your mother has outsmarted us all."

"But . . . but maybe the *last*," I said, nodding, sniffling.

"If only she had misbehaved," the lawyer said, shaking his head.

"*That* wasn't Mother," I said bitterly. "That was Mother playing a part." Like Joan of Arc going bravely to be burned. "What happens now?"

The elderly lawyer shrugged his slight shoulders. "We wait for sentencing."

"Which could mean her getting, what . . . ?"

He swallowed thickly. "Anywhere from twenty years to life."

"But she could get out *earlier*. . . ."

He nodded. "Yes. Yes, indeed. With good behavior."

Well, that nixed Mother.

Mr. Ekhardt stood, a shade wobbly. He patted my near shoulder. "I'll be in touch, child," he said.

I sat there a while longer, all alone in the courtroom, just me and that lucky blissfully ignorant baby inside me. I was trying to imagine life at home without Mother, and suddenly felt very small. Like little Brandy, when Mother would be taken away for a while to get well.

But she always came back.

Not this time. . . .

Outside the courtroom the gray-and-white marbled corridor yawned vacant. I walked along glumly, past hanging portraits of bygone politicians and presidents, their eyes seeming to follow me, their expressions unpitying.

At the top of the ornate circular staircase that led down into the rotunda, a woman stepped from behind a pillar, like the assasin who shot Huey Long. Had she been waiting for me?

In her late forties, or early fifties—professionally dressed in a brown linen skirt and jacket, sensible beige pumps, and a bulging bag hanging on a strap from one shoulder—she gave a small, tentative wave. Her large, intelligent eyes, straight nose, and wide mouth were framed by the soft curls of chin-length light brown hair.

I was in no mood to talk to anyone, and my face must have registered as much, because she gently asked, "Brandy? Brandy Borne?"

"Yeah."

She extended a hand to be shook. "Judith Meyers."

I shook it, the name registering. This was a longtime mental health advocate, who worked closely with NAMI (The National Alliance on Mental Illness). I had consulted her by phone, e-mail, and letter on various occasions about Mother.

I said, "Judith. Nice to finally meet you." Not that it really was under these circumstances. "Don't you live in Cedar Falls . . . ?"

"I do. But I try to keep track of all regional cases, particularly those that get on the NAMI radar. And this one sure did."

"I'd imagine."

"I thought maybe you could use a little support about now."

Two hundred and fifty miles was a long way to come. I said, "I didn't see you in the courtroom. . . ."

"I slipped in a little late."

I tried not to sound ungrateful. "Then you heard Mother plead guilty, so you must know there's really nothing you—or any of us—can do."

Her small smile gave a glimpse of straight white teeth. "Actually, there might be."

"Really?"

She nodded. "I think I might be able to offer considerable help. Is there somewhere we can go? Grab some coffee, perhaps?"

Was it possible Judith Meyers could succeed where Mr. Ekhardt had failed? Could she help get Mother off, or at least get her sentence reduced? Maybe these were straws I was grasping at, but I was ready to grasp away. . . .

I said, "There's a diner-type joint over in the next block that shouldn't be busy right now."

"Great! Lead the way."

We walked down the wide, curved marble staircase together. Though I'd never met the woman before, not in person anyway, her presence was enormously reassuring.

The Manhattan Restaurant, located on the first floor of a Victorian brick building on a side street kitty-corner from the courthouse, had been in business since Mother wore diapers (and I don't mean adult diapers, either).

The Manhattan's core clientele were those with a short lunch hour who worked at the courthouse, city hall, the county jail, and the police and fire departments . . . all within a three-block radius. So current owner, Pepe Kossives, employed no cute young waitresses who would encourage loitering, rather middle-aged ladies in uniforms and hair nets, who marched up and down the aisles like prison matrons, making sure you chowed down and got out. Still, there was always a line of people waiting to get in (especially when chicken and noodles were on special), and such strict measures were mandatory.

The layout was typical for a downtown Victorian building—boxcar-style with the original high tin ceiling (painted burgundy) and ceiling fans. There were a few high-backed wooden booths, and some tables and chairs; gray carpet covered the old pine floor. Along one wall was a long counter with stools, for those too impatient to wait for a table.

The front window displayed a two-foot-high statue of Wimpy, Popeye's pal from the comic strip by Elzie Segar (an Illinois native, just across the river). Naturally, the statue—which had been in that window since the 1930s—had Wimpy eating a hamburger. Once Mother tried to buy the precious collectible from Pepe, but he said that his grandfather had told him that if Wimpy was ever removed from the window, the restaurant would fall on hard times.

Once, a hooligan (long enough ago for him to still be called a hooligan) smashed the front window and stole Wimpy. (No, not Mother! She may have been a confessed murderer, but she was no thief.) Pepe was so inconsolable, the whole police department (who always got their coffee free at the Manhattan) went on unpaid overtime until the perpetrator was caught and Wimpy returned to his time-honored place.

I realize the previous paragraphs were a sizeable digression, even for me, but I share them with you because (a) I find the Manhattan and its history interesting, and (b) the first part of my conversation with Judith Meyers was a recounting of this same material. I was clearly trying to get my mind off the arraignment.

Judith and I settled into one of the high-backed wooden

booths. Other than two men in business suits deep in conversation over cups of coffee, we had the place to ourselves. One of those jail matrons in a navy dress uniform
(no hair net) came over and we both ordered iced tea. A
ceiling fan droned above us, providing some semblance of
cool air.

While we were waiting for our drinks, and I was rattling
on about Wimpy and hooligans and free coffee for cops,
Judith dug in her overstuffed bag, and began pulling out
papers, placing them on the table between us.

"First of all," she said, her voice lowered for privacy,
"I'd like to talk to you about your mother's rights—rights
by state law that protect the mentally afflicted while they
are incarcerated. For example, she has the right to see her
psychiatrist, to receive her medication—"

"What if Mother refuses her so-called 'rights'?"

"Then it's important for *you* to understand them, so
that she can still receive the best care possible."

Good. That made sense.

The waitress brought our drinks, and trundled off (others can trundle in this book—it's just me who isn't allowed).

I said, "I can tell you for certain that Mother won't go
back on her medication . . . but she does love to blab and
blather at her psychiatrist—he's from India, and has a lot
of patients *and* patience."

Judith took a sip of her iced tea, then said, "Well, that's
one thing we have going for us. Having a psychiatrist
monitor her mental condition is *very* important—especially for documentation."

"How so?"

"I'm sure your attorney is preparing to contest that
guilty plea, based upon your mother's past history . . . but
he will need your help. Do you think your mother would

sign a form giving you access to her mental health records?"

"She has in the past—several years ago. Is that one still good, d'you think?"

Judith shook her head. "You'll need a new one signed." She tapped the papers on the table. "There's one in here I can leave with you—along with a list of minimum requirements for mental health services in jail."

"Thanks." I pulled the papers over to my side of the table. "You're a lifesaver."

"That's an exaggeration, but you're welcome. Now your lawyer . . . what was his name?"

"Wayne Ekhardt."

"Mr. Ekhardt will want her to stay *off* the meds in order to have a stronger case."

I nodded, my eyes wide. "I can see why sometimes families and lawyers can be at odds."

"Which is why monitoring by a psychiatrist is so very important. If your Mother's mental health deteriorates too much, she could suffer, and you don't want that."

Judith and I talked a while longer, until our waitress gave us the evil eye because the lunch hour was approaching. Then I paid the check, and we parted ways, each pledging to stay in touch.

Since I had left my car on Main Street in front of the Laurel Building, I took a shortcut through the back alley of the restaurant.

Halfway down the alley, I became aware of a car behind me, and moved over to let it pass. A black Lincoln Town Car with heavily tinted windows rolled slowly alongside me, then stopped.

A window powered down to reveal a female driver. "Senator Clark wishes to speak to you," she said.

This was a woman with almond-shaped dark eyes and

straight black hair with bangs, cut chin-length, her scarlet red lipstick making a striking contrast against flawless skin, and matching the long red nails of her hands, which gripped the wheel. The top part of her—which was all I could see—was clothed in a tailored navy jacket over a cream-colored lace camisole.

The Lincoln's rear door opened, revealing Senator Edward Clark himself, his hand on the handle.

A crummy alley was *not* where I had imagined meeting my biological father for the first time.

He gestured for me to climb in. I debated whether or not I should accept this invitation, but finally I did.

You probably know from TV what the senator looked like—about sixty, movie-star handsome. Hollywood might have cast Paul Newman to play this elder statesman, with his silver hair, tanned face, and sky-blue eyes. But Paul Newman was gone, and I had only the genuine article, outfitted in an expensive gray suit and white shirt with cuffs.

Anyway, he didn't look *exactly* like Paul Newman. His facial features sort of looked like . . .

. . . mine.

He bestowed a disarming smile, showing teeth so perfect they surely were capped. "I've been trying to reach you since coming to town, Brandy—may I call you Brandy?"

My response was stilted and lame. "It's my name."

He went smoothly on. "But you either haven't been home, or you weren't answering the cell number Peggy Sue gave me." His eyes went to the back of the driver's head. "Denise . . ."

The woman turned; her gaze couldn't have been colder if carved from granite.

"Brandy, this is Denise Gardner, my top aide."

We nodded at each other.

"Denise, I need to speak to Ms. Borne privately. Please step out of the car for a few minutes, would you?"

She reacted, for just a split second, as if she'd been slapped; then she nodded again, and got out. Didn't slam the door or anything. She walked down the alley, folded her arms, then turned her back to us.

"Now we can speak freely," he said.

"What is it you want, Senator?"

The smiled faded a little. "Why, to meet you, of course."

In a dark alley?

"You mean," I said, "to find out if I'm *really* your daughter? Well, for that, you need a DNA test."

Or a mirror.

I dug into a pocket of my yellow dress and withdrew the tissue I'd used in the courtroom, tossing it on the seat between us. "Maybe you can get something out of that," I said.

He appeared hurt. "I can understand your hostility, Brandy . . . but you need to know that *I* didn't know Peggy Sue had gotten pregnant. You simply *must* believe me."

I said nothing.

He went on. "I was young, and made a terrible mistake. If I had known Peggy Sue had conceived, I promise you that I would have done the right thing."

"You mean, married her? Or arrange an abortion? In which case, we wouldn't be having this conversation, I guess. Kind of fitting we're talking in a back alley, though."

The senator didn't miss a beat. "I wouldn't have married her. I wasn't in love with Peggy Sue . . ."

Wow! An honest politician.

". . . and abortion is against my religious and personal beliefs. But I *would* have taken financial responsibility for you and her. And you would have had me in your life, as a father. A part-time father, but a father."

I said, "It's too late to talk about fatherhood, Senator. Not when my mother—I should say, my grandmother—will probably go to prison for the rest of her life because she wanted to protect your dirty little secret."

"But what about *you*, Brandy?"

I grunted a nonlaugh. "You want my assurance that I won't say anything? Well, don't worry. I don't want the embarrassment or the grief."

"No, that isn't what I meant. I . . . I'd like to get to know you better."

I shook my head. "You don't know me at all." I reached for the door handle. "Excuse me. Sorry. I have to go."

And I got out.

Denise heard the car door shut, wheeled. The aide's sky-high tan heels seemed as inappropriate as the short navy skirt. As I was exiting the alley, she stepped forward, blocking my path. She grasped my arm, her clawlike nails digging in.

"The senator has spent a lifetime building his career," she said sotto voce, to keep my father from hearing. "You better understand that I will *not* see it ruined."

She may have been excluded from our private conversation in the car, but she knew *something*.

"Let go," I said, wrenching away, the sharp nails scratching my skin.

"Call it a friendly warning," she whispered.

What I said in response was neither friendly nor fit for publication.

I backed away as the aide, heels clicking on brick, returned to the Town Car and resumed the driver's seat. In another moment the vehicle was speeding off down the alley. I watched, wondering just how far the aide would take her "friendly warning."

And I had to wonder whether the good senator had given up on fooling around with attractive female staffers.

A Trash 'n' Treasures Tip

For a novice collector, the best place to get the look of what authentic antiques are like is by visiting an exhibit at a museum or other facility. Look but don't touch, however—I found out the hard way that a busted Weller vase can set you back a couple hundred bucks.

Chapter Five

Knock-knock, Who's There? Mother. Oh, Brother!

Ah, my dearest ones! This is Vivian Borne speaking, or should I say writing, or better yet *communicating*, because that is, after all, my speciality—communication at its most forceful, direct and succinct.

As my darling daughter Brandy allots me only one measly chapter per book (in *Antiques Flee Market* I was granted two, but again she has cut me back to a meager one, perhaps because I have upstaged her), this is my moment to set things straight, and defend myself.

In our first book, *Antiques Roadkill*, Brandy explained to me "point of view"—or POV as we novelists refer to it. She had told me that when I write my chapter, I am to remain in my own head. Now I ask you, *Who else's head would I be in?*

But to be fair, Brandy did point out something valuable and important about mystery novels: a who-done-it cannot be written from the *murderer's* POV, because the reader would immediately know that the protagonist, often the very narrator, is the killer.

(Agatha Christie once broke this rule, and to this day there are those who criticize her for cheating. One can only wonder if Miss Christie might have been more successful had she played by the rules.)

So, let's get *that* out of the way!

Yes, I stabbed Connie. With the knife. I freely and fully admit it.

There is, however, one small detail that I must keep from you, dear reader. And I will accomplish this by simply *not thinking about it* while in my point of view! *Not thinking* is difficult, I admit, but I believe I can manage it. . . .

Upon my arrival at the county jail—a new state-of-the-art brick building conveniently located across from the courthouse, meaning hardly anybody ever escapes en route to an arraignment—I was first placed in what they call a pod: a separate area to determine whether or not I was mentally capable of joining the rest of inmate population.

Well, of course I was capable! It's not as if I'm deranged. Merely artistic.

Then, after my arraignment (little pregnant Brandy looked so sad that it almost broke my heart!), I was given my very own cell on the third floor, which was restricted to the female prisoners. The room was small but clean. There was a single bed (not too hard), a stainless-steel toilet and sink with mirror (not glass), and several shelves for storage.

A window—sans bars because it was too small for anyone to climb through (even Billy Buckly) (more about him later)—was nonetheless large enough to have some lovely sunshine stream in during the morning (vitamin D is so very important).

You may not realize this, but a great deal of thought goes into the sparse furnishings of a cell, due to various security issues. I would imagine there is some individual who goes around visiting cells, trying to hang him- or herself, or cut him- or herself, or perhaps pry something up to use against a guard.

And should he / she succeed, that element is changed or removed. Maybe his / her occupation even has a name, perhaps Prison Cell Checker-Outer . . . which I think would be a marvelous line of work. Unless, of course, one managed to hang oneself.

But I digress.

In the county jail (hereafter referred to as CJ), the inmates wear identical garb, both men and women: orange short-sleeved V-neck top and matching pull-on slacks (elastic waistband, thank goodness), plus orange slip-on sneakers.

Years ago I had my skin and hair coloring evaluated, and it turned out that I was a "Fall," meaning that I should wear clothing in the autumn color palette. And *nothing* says "fall" better than bright orange! Now I ask you, how lucky is that?

Bragging rights: I was responsible for this lovely new facility, because after I had landed in the crumbling, bug-infested old CJ on two occasions—once for trying to stop the destruction of one of Serenity's historic buildings, later for driving through a cornfield to make curtain time, hitting a cow (accidentally)—I vowed to campaign for a new jail, just in case I continued to now and then vacation there.

So! My hard work had paid off—although I felt sure that after my sentencing, I'd be heading off to the Big House (as they say in the cinema), because few inmates remain in CJ for more than a year. But until then, I would have it pretty cushy. Three hots and a cot!

The first night in my cell was moderately pleasant if uneventful. I had decided to scratch a mark on the cement wall by my bed for each day that I had spent here, to keep track of the time; but that ever-crafty "Prison Cell Checker-Outer" had done his / her job well, because I could find nothing around me that would make even the slightest scratch.

But he / she had not counted on Vivian Borne being in residence, because I was able to use my eyeglasses (the end thingamabob that goes around the ears) to accomplish my purpose.

I had also thought it would be apropos to print the words "Vivian was here" (a variation of the classic "Kilroy was here") in some discreet place, so as to lift the spirits of the cell's next inhabitant, and perhaps bring a smile to an unfortunate face. I was forced to abandon this project, however, as I was afraid of breaking my glasses with all that scratching, and I'm blind as a bat without them.

After lights out that first night, I lay on my small bed and began to sing, "Nooooo-body knows de trubble ah seen," which I thought was appropriate and a really nice touch.

But apparently not everyone on the cell block agreed, because I only made it to "mah sorrow" when one of the women rudely shouted for me to shut the fudge up. (I have substituted a word to protect you from the harshness of jailhouse vocabulary, but the more worldly among you may be able to see through my subterfuge.)

Amazingly, several other inmates shouted agreement to this nasty sentiment, which I thought was wholly inappropriate (we're not animals in cages, after all!). Still, as far as music goes, some people just don't appreciate spirituals. Perhaps one of the modern classics would do the trick.

But when "Jailhouse Rock" brought a similar reaction from a few more women, I gave up. If they didn't like the King, there was little use trying.

The next day I was able to meet my other roommates for the first time during recreation period in the common room. I wasn't at all nervous because I had watched every episode of the Australian soap *Prisoner: Cell Block H,* plus the British prison drama *Bad Girls,* so it was not as though I was a novice to life behind bars.

The first thing I decided to do was find out who the Top Dog was—usually the toughest-looking prisoner, or the one who'd been inside the longest—because I certainly didn't want to step on the wrong toes and wind up with a shiv in my side. Not on my first day!

So you can imagine my surprise when I approached a middle-aged husky woman with a crew cut, seated at one of the picnic-style tables, and received only a vacant stare in response to my Top Dog query.

A young, rail-thin blonde next to her answered with a frown, "There ain't no dog at the top or anywhere else, far as I know. They don't allow no pets in here."

"I don't mean a literal dog, dear—a *figurative* one."

"Huh?"

My goodness, no Top Dog? What kind of rinky-dink jail *was* this, anyway?

I tried again. "Well, dear, for goodness' sakes—how do you get anything *done* around here? Without a Top Dog, who is it that settles squabbles between the inmates, and negotiates with the screws?"

"The whats?"

"The screws, dear. The *guards?*"

The young woman merely shrugged; but I could tell by her wide-eyed expression that she was impressed by my knowledge of incarceration protocol. She introduced herself as Jennifer, just her first name, saying she was serving nine months for Controlled Substances (using, not selling) (this seemed to be a point of pride).

I stuck out my hand. "Vivian, Felony Murder. Nice to meet you."

When her crew-cut friend remained sullen and silent, Jennifer gestured, "This is Carol. Assault."

In an effort to draw shy Carol out of her shell, I asked, "Aggravated, serious, or simple?" I knew only too well the classes of misdemeanors from my past sentences.

Carol said glumly, "Aggravated . . . I'm stuck in here for another two months." Then she added bitterly, as if still tasting this morning's overly dry hash (a definite possibility), "But the b-word deserved it."

(She did not say "b-word." Again, I am taking the liberty of protecting the more delicate among you. Just because I am now a hardened veteran of the penal system does not mean I have lost my sensitivity.)

Sympathetically I said, "I'm sure she did, my dear." No sense in getting on the wrong side of Aggravated Assault.

By that time, the other three inmates seated at another table decided to come over and join our little kaffeeklatsch (minus coffee).

Jennifer made the introductions. There was Sarah—mid-twenties, tall, shapely, with shoulder-length red hair and green eyes—serving time for Bank Embezzlement; Angela—thirties, dark complected, short curly black hair, pudgy—third offense Drunk Driving; and Rhonda—either a well-preserved forty or hard-living thirty, long brown hair, attractive but for a bad complexion—Burglary.

With yours truly, we made a cozy group of six, which was about the usual number of female inmates for our size community.

Jennifer was gesturing to me. "And this is—" Getting caught up in making all those introductions, she had forgotten my name.

"Vivian, dear."

"This here is Vivian Deer—she's in for Murder."

Sarah tossed her red hair back from her face. "Good

riddance I say—I used to wait on Connie Grimes at the bank—*horrible* woman, so *rude. . . .*"

My reputation had preceded me!

Carol was nodding her short-cropped head. "Yeah, that fat cow would always roll her eyes when me and my partner'd walk by—like we was disgusting. What? And she *wasn't?*"

Angela chimed in. "My parents, they own El Burro? Once that *puta* complain about the food, then leave without paying the bill. But she eats her whole plate of enchiladas first, doesn't she?"

Only burglar Rhonda had nothing to add to the rather vivid word picture of the late Constance Grimes.

I patted the air with my hands. "Now, now, girls, it's not *polite* to speak ill of the dead. Everyone has *some* good in them . . . although I am hard-pressed to think of anything good to add about the deceased, at this time. If something occurs to me, you'll be the first to know."

Everyone fell silent for a moment, then Jennifer's face brightened like a child handed an ice cream cone. "Say, Vivian—why don't *you* be our Top Dog? I mean, since we ain't got one and you seem to know so much about it."

I patiently waited for protestations from the others, but none came. Just as I was experiencing a rush of pride, I noticed that Rhonda was staring at me with open hostility.

(I had never met the woman before, and could only think that some folks have difficulty adjusting to life behind bars.)

Nonetheless, I said, "Why, ladies, I'd be *honored.*"

Imagine, only my third day in stir and my first day on the cell block, and already I was Top Dog!

But something bothered me, and I touched a finger to my lips.

"You know," I ventured, "I don't much like the term

Top Dog—it sounds too negative, and I'm all about accentuating the positive, as you've surely noticed. Why don't you all call me 'Mother,' and I'll look out for you as if you were my very own."

Carol snorted, "Well, *my* mom was a—"

(In a way I regret not being able to report what Carol said next, because she did have a most unusual and graphic mode of self-expression, but our editor informs us that inclusion of same might cause this book to be excluded from several major chains. And Brandy and I are not writing these books for our health!)

I touched Carol's shoulder (I was still standing; she seated) and said, "Then allow me to be the *good* Mother that you never had."

That was a trifle clichéd, perhaps, but all clichés bear a kernel of truth, which is why it brought tears to Carol's eyes, and several of the others (if not Rhonda).

And to make good on my promise, I turned and marched across the room, right over to the Plexiglas window, behind which sat a female deputy at a bank of surveillance monitors, and pressed the intercom button.

"Patty," I said cordially, "would you please inform Sheriff Rudder that *Vivian Borne* would like to speak to him most urgently."

Patty—a woman in her forties, rather plain-faced, with dishwater blond short hair and no real enthusiasm for living (I knew her from the *old* CJ)—pressed a button on her side of the glass. *"What about, Vivian?"*

Which caught me a little off guard because I hadn't quite thought about *why* I wanted to see the sheriff, since I was really just trying to assert my Top Doggedness.

But I managed to reply, as if she should have known, "About the jail *conditions,* of course!"

Behind the Plexiglas, Patty's eyes closed. Had she fallen asleep?

I put my hands on my hips. "You know it's just as easy to serve *natural* applesauce as *sugared* . . . and why can't we ladies have a few Pilates balls in here? All that fattening food is going straight to our hips."

Due to the thick Plexiglas, I couldn't tell whether Patty was smiling or smirking at my requests (at least she'd opened her eyes again). But she didn't answer, merely clicked off her end of the intercom and turned her back to me.

But I had asserted myself and shown the others that I was serious about being their leader.

On the way back to join my new family, I had one of my usual strokes of genius (at my age, the only stroke worth having). Instead of wasting our recreational time watching soppy soap operas, or assembling jigsaw puzzles lacking the occasional piece, why couldn't we put on a play? Granted, the other women most likely had no acting experience whatsoever, but I possessed enough talent to carry us all.

To start with, we could learn a simple one-act play (with me in the lead role, of course), then perform it for Sheriff Rudder and his deputies, and finally to all of the other CJ inmates (the males). I had dozens of plays locked up in my head, so we didn't even need scripts.

(I immediately thought of *The Vagina Monologues*, but on further consideration, that piece might not be advisable for presentation to an abstinent male population.)

I was about to share my exciting new idea with my girls when Patty's voice came over the intercom.

"Vivian?"

I turned toward the Plexiglas. My, that was quick! Unlike Chief Tony Cassato, who always left me cooling my heels at the station, Sheriff Rudder never kept Vivian Borne waiting (perhaps preferring to take his medicine and get it over with).

But Patty announced, *"You have a visitor."*

The deputy jailor came out of the booth, then electronically unlocked the steel door to the common room, so that she could escort me to the visitor's station.

We went through another set of electronically locked doors, and then entered a small room (one of three identical separate cubbyholes) which was only large enough for me to be seated at another Plexiglas window. The deputy took her position behind me, by the door.

Across the barrier sat Brandy, alone in her small room, the child looking sad and pale, her peach-colored blouse only adding to her pall. (She should have had her colors done!)

I gave Brandy my best curtain-encore smile to reassure her that I was fine, then reached for my phone, saying into the receiver, "Dear, it's so nice of you to come."

"How are you doing, Mother?" Brandy asked, concern furrowing her brow. On my end, her voice sounded brittle and faint, like long distance in the olden days, but that could just be my bum ear.

"Why, I'm jim-dandy! No need to worry about me, dear." And I proceeded to tell her about my clean and comfortable room, and how I had already made friends with the other women.

(I thought it best to leave out becoming Top Dog, because Brandy had also watched *Bad Girls* with me, which included the episode where the Top Dog got strangled with a bedsheet by a jealous Top Dog wannabe.)

She was saying, "I had a meeting with Mr. Ekhardt this morning, and he thinks that if you change your plea to 'not guilty,' he could cut a deal with the DA, and—"

"Brandy! I'm *not* changing my plea. I *am* guilty. Please accept that, dear. I've had a good, long life on the outside and, actually, I'm quite happy in here."

Brandy looked appalled. "*Happy?* How can you be happy? You're in prison, Mother!"

All my years of preaching to be a "do bee," not a "don't bee," had never quite stuck with the girl.

I said patiently, "It's not prison, it's jail, darling. And I'm happy because there's so much I can accomplish 'on the inside.' "

"Like *what?*"

"Like starting a theater club among the women. We'll perform one-acts to begin with, then, eventually, complete three-act plays. And, who knows, maybe one day we'll be ready to tackle the Bard of Avon himself! '*Once more into the breach, dear friends!*' . . . Dear, a gaping mouth is not an attractive look at *any* age."

"You can't be *serious.* . . ."

"When am I ever *not* serious, dear? Why, we could take our productions on the road, performing at *other* prisons—state-wide at first—Anamosa, Fort Dodge, Newton." I raised a finger to make my point. "But *then* comes the big-time, Folsom, Leavenworth, San Quentin—and the *Broadway* of prisons . . . Sing Sing." I frowned. "Too bad Alcatraz is closed—how I would have *loved* to play there!"

Brandy was touching a hand to her forehead as if she didn't feel well and needed to take her own temperature. That girl really should take better care of herself. Didn't she realize she was pregnant?

"Dear," I said, "would you mind if we cut this short? I want to get back and tell the other girls all about my playcraft plans."

Brandy sighed. "I'm sure you do, Mother. All right. I'll go."

"And get some rest—you look *terrible.*"

I hated to give Brandy the bum's rush, but recreation time in the common room was almost over.

By the time Patty escorted me through the two security doors, however, I'd missed my moment—my girls were already in lockdown. My theater proposition would just have to wait until dinnertime.

The meals in CJ—at least for the female inmates—were TV dinner affairs, wheeled in on a cart three times a day. One had no say, of course, on what was being served: what you saw was what you got . . . high in fat and low in taste. Stone walls may not a prison make, but atrocious, unhealthy food certainly does.

This evening was greasy meat loaf, watery mashed potatoes, and rubbery green beans, which I left untouched because I didn't want to waste my energy on such unappetizing fare. Instead, I wanted to propose my wonderful new idea to the others.

With our little group spread out at the two picnic tables, I stood and tapped my plastic spork against my paper cup of water, which wasn't nearly as effective as the classy resonant *ping* that sterling makes against crystal. Nonetheless, the girls all stopped eating, every eye on me.

With my usual theatrical flair, I launched into my brainstorm, outlining the theater program in great detail. And when I had finished, I was met with a stunned silence (which does happen sometimes after the curtain comes down on my stage performances—art can have that effect), so I wasn't too concerned.

But then, to my dismayed shock, came a gale of laughter. Well, dear reader, I felt like I'd been punched in the breadbasket! Fortunately, I hadn't been eating.

Almost immediately, Sarah came to my defense.

"Wait a minute!" the red-haired woman said. "A theater program might not be such a bad idea. Think about it, everybody! An opportunity to do something *different* around this boring dump."

"Yeah," chimed in blond Jennifer. "And maybe get out of this s-word-hole . . . even for a *little* while."

(Jennifer didn't say "s-word-hole," either. But I do regret having to omit it. After all, "s-h-i-t" is *my* favorite expletive!)

Pudgy Angela offered eagerly, "In high school? When the guy who was supposed to play Sancho Panza in *Don Quixote* got sick? *I* did that role . . . so I can play male parts okay."

"Me, too," said crew-cut Carol with a shrug. "In fact, I prefer it."

I beamed at my new children; they had not let their mother down.

A possible exception, however, was Rhonda, who remained her usual silent, sullen self. (Didn't she know those frown lines would become permanent, making her poor complexion even more problematic?)

"What about *you,* my dear?" I asked her, trying to draw the woman out and in. "Any experience trodding the boards?"

The frown lines became smirk lines. "If you mean acting in a *play* . . . then, no, thank God. I don't want anything to do with your stupid, harebrained idea."

Sarah once again rode to my rescue. "What's eating you, Rhonda? You've been *terrible* to Vivian—I mean, Mother—ever since she got here! What's your problem?"

Rhonda rose from the table, her face flushed with fury, and pointed a finger right at me, like Uncle Sam in full recruitment mode. "*I'll* tell you what my problem is! It's *her* fault I'm *in* here!"

I looked quizzically at the woman. "I don't understand, my dear. How can I possibly be responsible for your incarceration? I don't even know you. We had never met before today."

Rhonda came around the table to plant herself next to me, jabbing my chest with the finger. "You batty old bat. *I* was robbing the house across the street from the Grimes woman when all the cops came around . . . and they caught me!" She jabbed some more. "So it's *your* damn fault!"

"Well, my dear," I answered cooly, "perhaps you should have been more careful in your chosen profession. . . ."

And I grabbed her finger, twisting it back until she yelped.

(This might not have been wise, but as I learned from *Bad Girls,* the Top Dog must never lose face or back down, least she be found strangled with a bedsheet. And, anyway, the finger-twist had worked very effectively for Bea on *Prisoner: Cell Block H.*)

Luckily, before the altercation went any further, Patty's voice sounded over the intercom. "*Vivian! Sheriff Rudder wants to see you!*"

Which only confirmed my position as Top Dog . . . that is, Mother Hen.

Rhonda retreated to her table where she sat, defeated, nursing a sore finger. Sometimes children need a firm hand (perhaps I should have tried that with Brandy).

Jennifer called out, "Hey, Mother—ask for some sci-fi paperbacks instead all this romance doody! I've read everything that's in here."

"And Sudoku puzzles," Sarah said. "I'm bored out of my gourd!"

Angela intoned, "And how about some Hispanic food once in a while—I mean, who *doesn't* like a taco?"

"I shall do my best," I promised. "Carol? Don't *you* have a request?"

She shook her head.

"Oh, come, now . . . surely there's something you want," I asked, as if coaxing a Christmas wish from an undecided child.

"Well," Carol said, staring at the floor, "I *would* like a book on gardening. 'Cause when I get out of this dump I'm gonna have one."

"Ah!" I said. "Very worthwhile *and* therapeutic. Vegetable or flower?"

"Herbal."

"All right then," I said to all of my children, clapping my hands once, "I'll do what I can."

"Vivian! *Now!*" Patty was standing just inside the common room, by the security door, her expression rather cross. At least her eyes were open.

This time she took me through three security doors to a room much larger than the cubbyhole visitor's station, but just as stark—cement block walls, tan tiled floor, one rectangular metal table (bolted down), and two chairs (similarly secured). On the wall near one chair was a shackle, to be used for the more dangerous inmates.

To my great surprise—and delight—there were two people waiting for me! Whatever had I done to deserve so much attention?

Next to Sheriff Rudder—a tall confident man who reminded me of Randolph Scott, except that his eyes were just a trifle crossed—was Chief Cassato! What luck that I should have such an audience for the presentation of my requests for prison improvement . . . and to pitch my theater program.

Patty deposited me in the chair next to the shackle, while Rudder and Cassato stood a short distance away behind the table. Rudder had on his usual tan pressed uniform with shiny sheriff's badge, while Cassato wore his version of a uniform—crisp white shirt, dark pants, and black wing-tipped shoes. Both wore stern expressions.

I said, "How good of you, Sheriff, to see me so promptly! And how nice of you, Chief, to drop by for a visit. I assume it's out of respect for all of the cases I've helped you clear up."

When neither man gave me even the teeniest of smiles, I pressed on. "I know you are both busy bees, so I won't take much of your—"

"Shut up," Sheriff Rudder said flatly.

Well, dear reader, I was quite taken aback by this rude outburst, and began to sputter protestations.

"I said, *be quiet!*" Rudder snapped. "Chief Cassato has something to say."

The chief leaned on the table, his bulk supported by fists. He smiled now, but it didn't seem very friendly.

"I got the autopsy report on Connie Grimes back from the DCI today," he said, then cocked his bucket head. "Interested?"

"Not particularly," I said. I was studying my nails. I really could use a manicure. . . .

Still, I glimpsed the chief's smile turning nasty. "*Really?* Vivian Borne not interested in confidential police reports . . . ?" He laughed but it seemed to me rather forced. "That's a new one." He leaned even closer. "Could that be because you already *know* what the autopsy showed?"

"I have no idea what you could be referring to," I said innocently. The back of my neck itched terribly and I just had to scratch it.

He slammed the tabletop with a fist.

I jumped a little.

"You don't, huh? Vivian, I now know what you've known all along—that Connie Grimes was *already dead* when you stabbed her!"

And that, precious one, is the small detail I kept from you by not thinking about it. I hope you'll forgive me this stratagem.

The chief was saying, "You found the Grimes woman dead with a knife in her chest. You removed it, wiped it for prints, and stabbed her yourself, leaving your prints behind to lead us astray."

"I plead the Fifth," I said.

Chief Cassato straightened. His chest was heaving. "Who are you protecting, Vivian?"

I said nothing.

Sheriff Rudder finally spoke. "Vivian, you're already in trouble. Please cooperate, before you get yourself in even more of a jam—who are you protecting?"

I stared at the shackle on the nearby wall.

Several interminable moments passed, then Chief Cassato said to Rudder, as if I were no longer present, "Well, she can't be covering for Brandy. *She's* in the clear."

Rudder turned to Cassato. "What about the other daughter—the Hastings woman? Peggy Sue?"

He shook his head. "Not a chance. Her story's been checked and rechecked."

Something must have flickered in my peepers, because Cassato suddenly leaned on the table again.

"But it *is* Peggy Sue, isn't it?" he asked.

"Yes! I, mean, no!" I blurted, then, "You're trying to *trick* me! I saw this on *Perry Mason!*"

Cassato came around the table, planting himself in front of me. "Vivian. Listen to me. Believe me. Peggy Sue is *not* a suspect. She has an unshakable alibi."

I felt my eyes growing wet. "I don't *believe* you. . . ."

The chief placed one hand on my shoulder, saying gently, "Peggy Sue was playing bridge at the country club all that morning—surely you knew that."

I nodded. "But . . . she could have *left* and come back."

The chief said, "She *didn't*. A dozen witnesses swear Peggy Sue remained at her bridge table the entire morning. Viv, she didn't even use the ladies' room."

"But . . . but . . . I saw—" I was about to say that I thought I'd seen Peggy Sue's car leaving Hidden Pines just as the trolley dropped me off . . .

. . . but thought better of it.

Cassato frowned. "Saw *what*, Vivian?"

I shook my head. "Nothing. I'm just a foolish old woman who hasn't been herself lately. Did you know I've been off my meds for some time?"

(Normally, I would never say such ridiculous things about myself, but I needed to end that line of conversation. After all, Peggy Sue was not a suspect, so I must have been wrong about seeing her car. Mustn't I?)

Whatever trouble I might be in personally, nonetheless a great relief washed over me, a carefree tide. I felt giddy, and began to weep and laugh all at once.

Tony Cassato gallantly offered me his handkerchief, which I used to wipe my eyes, then blow my nose, with an embarrassing Harpo-like honk.

"Excuse me," I said winsomely. I handed the hanky toward him.

"Keep it."

(Over the past few months Brandy had collected several of the chief's handkerchiefs, but this was my first.)

When I had composed myself, I asked, "What happens to me now?"

Sheriff Rudder said, "You'll be released, pending new charges."

That brought me to my feet. "*What?* That's ridiculous, just plain foolish. I'm here *now.* I've obstructed justice— tampered with a crime scene. I want to start serving my time!"

The chief sighed. "That isn't how the system works, Vivian. You have to go through due process again. And who knows, maybe you *won't* be back—maybe you'll get probation, community service. . . ."

"No! Book *me,* Danno! I insist! I'm guilty. Give me the longest *possible* sentence."

I had plays to produce!

Rudder looked behind me to Patty, who had been waiting quietly by the security door. "Get this Fruit Loop out of here."

That wasn't very nice at all!

Patty moved forward, and grasped me by an arm.

"Wait!" I said, digging my heels in. "I'm not finished yet. We women have demands—we need more nourishing food, better books, some exercise equipment, HBO—not just basic cable! And, uh . . . conjugal rights." I threw that last one in as a perk. It had been a big topic on *Bad Girls.*

"*Get her* out *of here!*" the sheriff hollered.

Patty had opened the security door and was dragging me through, but I grabbed on to the door's handle long enough to declaim, "I will be back! Don't think you've seen the last of Vivian Borne!"

Sheriff Rudder put one hand to his forehead. "I could always poke my eyes out," he said.

What an odd thing to say.

Mother's Trash 'n' Treasures Tip

Be wary of stories attached to antiques, sometimes used by a seller to enhance the value of an item. Like the tall tale I once fell for—"It belonged to President James Buchanan's second wife." Buchanan never had a *first* wife!

Chapter Six

Knock-about

The morning Mother was released from the county jail, I threw a little party for her at the house, inviting only Peggy Sue (and Sushi). I had baked a white sheet cake, slathered it with white frosting, then added black liquorice-stick jail bars, and red lettering reading: WELCOME HOME FROM THE POKEY. (I thought about putting a file in the center, but decided that might be a trifle unsanitary.)

The antique Duncan Phyfe table in the dining room was set with our best mismatched china, and at Mother's place, I'd set a Monopoly "Get out of jail free" card.

Peggy Sue, wearing her signature Burberry (a pink-and-tan plaid cotton shirtdress), did not seem particularly taken with these festivities . . . but Mother whooped with glee when I conveyed the cake in from the kitchen ("Ta *dah!*").

Just in case any of us had avoided a sugar coma from the sweet dessert, I also served chocolate mint ice cream (Mother's favorite) and tart lemonade.

Peggy Sue and I were so thrilled that the murder charges against Mother had been dropped, neither she nor I felt much like reprimanding her. I'm sure, however, at a later date, Sis and I would have our scolding say.

For now, we were all smiles at the table, happy to have among us again our very own jailbird (a cuckoo joke here would be pushing it, don't you think?).

Peggy Sue was saying, "Mom, I'm sorry to get into such unpleasantness when we're having such a nice homecoming . . . but why in heaven's name did you think *I* had killed Connie?"

Mother, in the process of slipping a morsel of cake under the table to a begging Sushi, replied, "Because, dear, I thought I saw your car leaving Hidden Pines when the trolley dropped me off, which was about the time that awful woman was murdered . . . may she rest in peace. And you certainly had a motive to rid the world of Connie Grimes."

Peggy Sue wasn't about to go into that. Instead she just shrugged it off, saying, "Well, mine isn't exactly the *only* blue Escalade in town, you know—that's a very popular model."

Otherwise she wouldn't own it.

"Besides," Peggy Sue went on, stiffening a little, "I can't help but be offended that you could *ever* imagine that I am the kind of person who'd do such a . . . a *brutal* thing. Now, if you'd thought it was *Brandy*—"

"Thank you so very much!" I said. I was almost wishing I'd put that file in the cake and let Sis bite her perfect teeth down on it.

Mother's fork, loaded with cake, dripping in green-chocolate ice cream, paused on its path to her mouth. "Are you *sure,* dear, that your car wasn't *taken* while you were playing bridge?"

I spoke. "You mean, as in stolen, used maybe to implicate Peg, then returned? That's a little far-fetched, isn't it, Mother?"

Mother, chewing, said, "I've seen that kind of thing

happen on *Perry Mason* any number of times. And in Rex Stout, Agatha Christie, and—"

"Any *real-life* examples, Mother?" I asked, too dignified to speak with my mouth full, even if I had spilled ice cream on the front of me.

But Sis was waving all of this away. "Impossible," she said, declaring herself the final word on the subject. "The car was in the exact same spot as when I first parked it . . . and the lot was full that morning. Don't you think I would have *noticed* if it had been moved?"

Well, I guess she had a point. Still, *I* wouldn't have noticed if *my* car had been moved, being the sort of person who wanders parking lots, forced to use my car's security alarm to make my vehicle call out to me. *Honk,* over *here* you imbecile, *honk, honk.* . . .

Mother said, "Well, I would have bet my life that it was your car."

"You did," I pointed out. But I was getting impatient with Mother's persistence on this matter, and asked, "If you're so sure, does that mean you saw the license plate, and recognized it as Peggy Sue's?"

"Well . . . no."

I pressed. "Did you get a look at the driver? Was it a woman, maybe with the same hair color as Peg, and that was what made you so certain?"

"Well . . . no."

"Then," I suggested, "let's just drop it. You're in the clear, Peggy Sue is in the clear, and I'm in the clear. And not to be too unkind, but the Connie Grimes problem is solved. So why go looking for trouble?" I raised my glass of lemonade. "Here's to the one-hundred-percent-not-guilty Borne girls!"

Later, as I walked with Sis to her car, she asked in a lowered voice, "Do you *really* think we're in the clear? I mean, about that *other* matter? Our relationship with the senator is *still* a volatile one."

Our relationship? I wasn't the cause here, I was the effect!

I said frankly, "I don't know. But we don't seem to be the only ones worried about it."

She came to a melodramatic halt and grasped my arm—a little of Mother's theatrics, apparently, had seeped in. "What do you mean, Brandy? *What* other ones are worried?"

I told her about my brief alley encounter with Senator Clark and his less-than-charming assistant, the timing of which had been directly after Mother's arraignment.

But she didn't seem at all surprised.

In fact, what she said was, "Do you blame him for keeping an eye on the situation?"

"You sound like . . . like you already knew about me talking to the senator."

"Yes," she said, then added rather acidly, "and I was embarrassed to hear about it."

"*You* were embarrassed?"

"That's right. Apparently you weren't very nice."

"You *are* my real mother, right? I wasn't dropped off on a porch by gypsies or anything?"

"Brandy . . . please . . ."

"So my ever-loving daddykins said I wasn't nice, huh? *When* did he tell you that?"

Her chin rose in that familiar I'm-not-just-anybody manner of hers. "Edward . . . Senator Clark . . . has been in town quite a bit lately. He's opened up a campaign office for this fall's election." She shrugged. "We've met several times."

I narrowed my eyes at her. "Is that so?"

"That's so." Now her eyes narrowed right back at me.

"And it's not what your dirty little mind is thinking. I've been . . . helping out some at the campaign office."

"Isn't that how this all started? Can I expect a baby sister in about nine months?"

"Brandy, that's outrageous!" she said. "It's cruel and uncalled for."

Cruel maybe.

"Besides," she went on, "that aide of his, Denise Gardner, is the keeper of the gates. She wouldn't allow anything . . . *inappropriate* . . . to take place, even if we wanted it to. She's very protective of the senator."

I gave up a grunt. "A real Dragon Lady, if you ask me. I can't tell whether she's more ambitious for her boss or herself."

"She is just doing her job," Sis said.

"Really? Maybe she doesn't want anything 'inappropriate' to happen between the senator and anybody else but *her.*"

"You have no basis to think that harshly of the senator!"

I patted my chest. "I *am* the basis for thinking that harshly of the senator! Listen, what if dainty little Denise figures that eliminating Connie Grimes fell under her job description?"

Sis look horrified. "You can't be *serious.* . . ."

I shrugged. "Senator Clark has a lot to lose if word got out that he was my father. And your lover, back when you were barely legal."

"Brandy, that's *terrible!*"

"Yeah. A lot of people would think so."

She swallowed thickly and her features softened. The argument was over. She touched my arm. "Brandy . . . you have to put this bitterness aside. We're all adults."

Now we're all adults, I thought. *When this started, you*

were just a teenager. But I didn't say it. I didn't want to fight anymore.

She said, barely able to get the words out, "Edward . . . Edward says he'd like to *see* you again."

"Does he."

"He felt awful about how your first meeting went. Listen, he's really a wonderful man. So very important."

Which pretty much was how Sis defined "wonderful": important.

But my heart softened when she pitifully asked, "Will you go see him, please . . . for me?"

I sighed. "When?"

"You will see him?"

"I said I would. When already?"

"I'll talk to him and get back to you."

Ever the senator's loyal staffer.

I just nodded.

"And give him a *chance*, Brandy . . . please? It wasn't all his fault."

I didn't know if she was referring to that unpleasant alley encounter, or my existence, and didn't feel like going into it. So I just gave her another sour little nod.

With renewed spring in her step, Sis went to her Caddy and got in behind the wheel of the status symbol, while I trudged back to the house.

Mother was in the kitchen, cleaning up after our party, Sushi lurking, sniffing the floor, on the prowl for any morsels that might have been dropped, accidently or on purpose.

I was standing at the counter, stuffing another piece of cake in my mouth (eating for two, remember!), when an idea struck me. There was no way Mother would not look into Connie's murder. Of that I was sure. But I could see a way to make that pay a very attractive dividend.

So I swallowed and said, "Mother, I know this won't be easy . . . but from here on out, you and I will *have* to stay out of this murder investigation."

Hand-washing a delicate china cup at the sink, Mother paused. "And why is that, dear?"

"Because all three of us—you and me and Peggy Sue— really *did* have a motive for killing Connie Grimes . . . and that motive might come to light."

"I see."

"So it's best that the police handle this—I mean Tony is an experienced detective, and under his leadership, even the most inept officers on the Serenity force should be able to rise to the occasion. Maybe they'll discover it was some burglar who was surprised to find the lady of the house home."

Mother turned abruptly away from the sink. "But a burglar *didn't* do it!"

"You sound certain of that."

"I am!"

Her conviction made me suspicious—she *knew* something. . . .

I pretended not to have noticed. "Well, it doesn't matter. Neither one of us is up to the job, anyway."

Mother huffed, "What ever do you mean? Not *up* to it? Since when were *we* not up to sussing out a murderer?"

"Well, in case you haven't noticed, I'm pregnant," I said, "and *you're* certainly not at the top of your game."

Mother's eyes flared behind the large lenses; it was like gas burners on a stove flaming on. "You will explain yourself, young lady! *Why* would you claim that I am not at the top of my game?"

Hands on hips, I said, "Okay, Mother, I'll tell you. You seem distracted, not able to focus—for example, are you even aware you've washed that cup twice already?"

A lie.

Mother frowned and examined the cup as if it were a moon rock. "Really?"

I nodded. "And at the table? You kept calling me Peggy Sue."

Another lie.

"No! Really?"

"Really," I said, matter of fact. "So you see, we wouldn't be of any use, either of us, trying find whoever killed Connie . . . which is too bad, because I bet it would be the juiciest case we ever solved."

With that, I vacated the kitchen for the living room, where I pretended to sort through mail that had collected on the Victorian tea table by the front door.

Mother appeared next to me, a bug-eyed apparition, saying, "You know, dear, I really *haven't* been my old self, lately. My thoughts race and I feel nervous all the time—sometimes I feel like I could just *jump* out of my skin."

She demonstrated this feeling with a spasmodic piece of clawing-at-the-air and running-in-place miming that would have startled Marcel Marceau into crying out in alarm.

Reading a piece of junk mail with intense interest, I said casually, "Maybe it would help your investigative abilities if you, I don't know, went back on your medication."

Mother was silent while I studied another solicitation. Then I turned and asked innocently, "Do you think it might help?"

Her frown made me wonder if she had seen through this don't-throw-me-in-the-briar-patch routine.

But her eyes widened and she shrugged and, *yes!*, she said, "I suppose it couldn't hurt."

Reining myself in, I responded at first with another round of silence, so very caught up in another piece of junk mail. Imagine—cheese-filled pizza crust! What would they think of next?

Then Mother said, timidly, tentatively, "Would you . . . would you be more inclined to drive me places, dear, if I took my medication? Not that I *need* it, of course, but you seem to think I do, and I do so like to please you."

Right.

She was saying, "And, of course, I *am* worried about *your* mental health. Mustn't have you in a scattered state with a little one on the way."

We were in full-sway negotiation mode now—no need for me to make counteraccusations.

I put down the advertising flyer I'd been reading, and picked up another. "Well, I think I would probably be inclined to drive you around just about any place you might want to go—within reason."

That should cement the deal, and still leave me wiggle room in case she wanted to visit Alcatraz to check it out as a possible performing venue.

"All right, dear, I'll go *back* on my medication," Mother said, with a firmness that suggested it had been her idea. Then she added, "Only, I'm afraid I threw the pill bottle in the trash several months ago."

"I dug it out," I said instantly. "It's in the medicine cabinet behind the laxatives."

Mother smiled wryly. "You are a resourceful child. You get that from me, you know."

"I know. Want me to get you a glass of water?"

"I can do that, dear." She knew she'd been had, but a deal was a deal. "You've done enough already."

Before we could begin our unofficial investigation into Connie's murder, Mother and I would first have to tend to our financial situation—specifically the payment of our ongoing lawyer's bill, which (even if Wayne Ekhardt *had* once been in love with Mother) could eventually become substantial. Realizing we were sitting on a small gold mine with our Acklin clock, we quickly agreed, if reluctantly, to sell it.

An eventful week or so had passed since we'd taken the clock in for repairs—all but forgotten in the wake of Mother's jailing—and now we headed to Mr. Timmons's shop to retrieve it, and get his advice on how to go about getting the best price for the rare antique.

Once again—coincidence or fate?—we ran into Mrs. Vancamp in the parking lot of the old funeral-home-turned-mall. But, the elderly woman did not look so chipper, her quick birdlike movements nonexistent, the tiny eyes red-rimmed behind the glasses, facial features sagging even more than usual. As before, she was carrying the bedside Acklin clock, but it was unprotected in her hands.

"That man said it was a fake, a knock-off!" she blurted as we drew near.

Mother asked, "What man, dear?"

"Mr. Timmons! I needed to sell it to pay my property taxes, but he told me my clock was worth less than one hundred dollars. That can't be! My husband wouldn't have bought an antique that wasn't authentic—he would have had it appraised first!"

And she began to cry.

Mother put an arm around the heaving shoulders of the sobbing old girl. "Now, now, dear . . . even an expert can be fooled by a really *good* knock-off. What you must remember is that your husband bought it for you with love. That makes it precious beyond dollars."

Mother glanced at me with embarrassment; even she knew that was over the top.

But Mrs. Vancamp nodded and sniffled. "I . . . I guess you're right, Vivian. And I *do* like the clock—it keeps perfect time—and Mr. Timmons *did* say that it was a very *good* knock-off."

Mother released the woman, cooing, "Let's not say 'knock-off,' dear. That has such a vulgar ring. Let's call it a 'reproduction,' shall we? Maybe it isn't worth much literally, but its sentimental value is priceless."

To me, Mother seemed about as convincing as a late-night cable pitchman. On the other hand, a lot of people call in and order that junk. . . .

"Yes, Vivian," Mrs. Vancamp said, nodding like a bobble-head doll, "I can see that you're right. I'm . . . I'm actually glad that I don't have to sell it. Now it will be with me always. Something I will treasure."

Even if it was trash.

We watched the woman slowly walk to her car, though the quirky birdlike movements seemed to be returning. Then Mother took my elbow.

"Let's go, dear."

"And give her some privacy?"

"No—escape before she runs us down in the parking lot."

In the backroom repair shop of the old funeral home, Mr. Timmons was working on a disassembled clock at one of the stainless-steel embalming tables. He looked up pleasantly as Mother and I entered.

But his cheerful expression dropped into a weary frown. From our expressions, he must have guessed we'd run in to the recently departed (from the mini-mall, not the earth) Mrs. Vancamp.

"You saw her?" the bearded little man asked, his brow making the kind of furrows that give birth to wrinkles.

I rolled my eyes and nodded, and Mother said, "Yes. It was a great blow to the poor soul to discover that her beloved clock was not an authentic Acklin." Then she added dramatically, "I did what I could to ease her sorrow. As a wise person once said, 'We are here for such a short span, it is incumbent upon us to lighten the load of our fellow beings.' "

I gave her a look. "Who said *that?*"

"Why, I did, dear. Just now."

Timmons sighed sadly. "I hated to tell her—it just broke her heart. But she shocked the heck out of me."

"How so?" Mother asked.

"She wanted me to buy the clock! I supposed she'd want to hold on to it, out of sentiment."

I said, "In tough times, sentiment's value drops faster than the dollar's."

Mother looked at me. "And who said that, dear?"

"I did. Just now." To the clock repairman, I said, "So you had to break it to her. You couldn't just say you weren't interested."

"No. Because if I didn't want to buy it, she'd have tried to sell it to someone else. And that meant either she'd be unwittingly misrepresenting it to another uneducated buyer, or some dealer would have delivered the bad news, and let her down much harder than I did."

"We understand, Ben," Mother said. "It was the right thing to do. Can't have a knock-off floating around out there." She shifted gears, having given sufficient time to someone else's problems. Mother has a lot of compassion, for an egocentric.

I said, "I hope you're not about to give us similar bad news about *our* Acklin . . ."

He smiled, stepping away from his work. "Not hardly!"

". . . because like Mrs. Vancamp, *we* want to sell ours."

"Oh . . . I thought you were planning to keep it."

"We were," I said, shrugged, and sighed, "but now it seems we'll have to sell it to pay Mother's lawyer's fee. You've seen the papers? I thought maybe the police would have been by to question you about our altercation last week. That's what spurred everything."

"I'm well aware of what's been happening, but actually, no, the police haven't stopped by." Timmons stepped to the counter that separated us. "As for your Acklin, I'd love to buy it . . . if we can arrive at an agreement on price. Afraid I'm also feeling the pinch of the economy these days. . . ."

I didn't like the way the conversation was heading, with us put in the position of soft-balling a figure, so I turned to Mother.

"Say," I said, "why don't we not put Mr. Timmons on the spot today? We can do some research on the Net and through some auction houses, and see what a similar Acklin mantel clock has gone for. Then, let's set a firm price and showcase it in our booth at the antiques mall. It won't sell, of course, but we can at least get some publicity out of it."

Mother's eyes began to dance behind her glasses. "Wonderful idea, dear. Think of how it will attract people to our booth! If they can't afford the clock, perhaps they'll buy something else. We *are* overstocked. And then perhaps we wouldn't have to sell the clock after all!"

Timmons didn't seem to care one way or the other. He just shrugged and said, "Well, it's your Acklin."

I smiled. "Yes, it is. May we have it, please?"

For some time now, Mother and I had been renting an antiques booth downtown in an old (as yet unrestored) Victorian four-story building at the end of Main Street. The purpose of our venture was (a) to clear out some of our clutter, (b) make a little mazuma, and (c) keep Mother out of trouble. All of which was working . . .

. . . except for "c."

The Victorian building, with its ornate facade and unique corner entrance, had a checkered reputation, several murders having taken place in the building, which did not seem to bother antiques hunters looking for a bargain.

The current owner, Ray Spillman, was a short, spry, slender fellow in his late seventies with thinning gray hair, a bulbous nose, and a slash of a mouth. After the most recent murder on the premises, he had asked Father O'Brien from St. Mary's to bless the building, and the hocus-pocus had worked—no further homicides . . . so far.

But the priest should have included a blessing against burglary, because the store had been broken into several times, inspiring Ray to install an expensive alarm system, the cost passed along to his booth renters. So all of us were doubly concerned about turning a good profit.

While Mother held a dim view of breaking and entering, she was pragmatic on simple customer booth thievery: if a person wanted something so badly as to conceal it in their purse or pocket, then they could have it. She was assuming, however, that the snitcher didn't have any money, and would take the item home and cherish it, which wasn't always the case, as sometimes our items wound up in one of Serenity's pawn shops.

Occasionally, however, items that disappeared were not stolen, just picked up and set down absentmindedly in another booth, when the customer decided against the purchase. Such was the case with our yellow smiley-face alarm clock (a bad purchase on my part, I admit), which I'd thought we'd finally gotten rid of, only to have it now staring back at me, as I surveyed our booth. Apparently, someone thought better of waking up to the silly grinning face.

Not much had sold since our last visit, August being a slow month for dealers. A few empty spots in the dust on the blue glass top of an Art Deco end table (display only) indicated some movement of inventory. Gone was a Fenton milk-glass candy dish, a Frankoma green vase, and a

Bugs Bunny drinking glass, items not valuable enough to have locked in our curio case, reserved for rare items like the Li'l Abner tin toy band, and a dress shield autographed by the older Frank Sinatra—Mother pushing her way backstage after a Midwestern concert, having a pen but no paper, and improvising as only she could.

While Mother was visiting with Raymond at the center circular checkout station, I dusted and straightened our booth, moving a few things around to make it look like we'd added new merchandise. Then, satisfied that I'd done what I could to make our little world enticing, I joined Mother.

She was informing Ray, "The Acklin clock will be in the curio cabinet. Please only show it to those who are serious about buying it—the less it's handled the better."

Ray, on the other side of the counter, with an ever-present bottle of Coke within easy reach, asked, "Firm price?"

"Yes," Mother said, adding, "It will be too rich for most people's blood, of course, but then we don't expect to sell it, rather to draw customers to our booth. We'll take the clock to auction, later. . . . Ah, Brandy!"

Mother had finally noticed me, and she gestured to the box with the carefully wrapped clock at her feet. "Bring the Acklin up on the counter where Ray can see it, will you, dear? My knees aren't what they used to be. . . ."

Neither were her elbows or shoulders, but the hips were fine, having been replaced. I didn't point out the difficulty of a pregnant woman bending over, not that it would have done any good.

After I'd unveiled the mantel clock before Ray's bright, shining eyes, the elderly man studied it carefully, stem to stern.

Finally he said, "This is a real find . . . a beautiful example of Acklin at his best. . . . Only . . ."

Mother and I frowned.

"Only what, Ray?" I asked first.

"I've never seen Acklin use anything but genuine gold for the face hands."

Mother and I leaned in simultaneously for a closer look, and bumped heads.

"That's not real gold?" Mother asked. "How can you tell?"

Ray had the clock's glass face-cover open and was gently wiggling the minute hand. "By the thickness and weight, Vivian. This is flimsy—brass or gold-plated, most likely."

Mother looked crestfallen.

I asked, "What will that do to its value?"

Ray shrugged his slight shoulders. "It *will* make a difference . . . but the rest of the clock appears authentic. You really won't know until it's appraised and taken to auction."

I could almost hear what Mother was thinking: *Let the buyer beware.* But I always found it better to be up-front about known flaws in an antique: deceit had a way of coming back and biting one on the derriere.

Ray had a customer now, a teenage boy buying a 1970s vintage comic book, so Mother and I collected our fine but flawed Acklin and headed back to our booth.

After positioning the clock on the top shelf of the curio, showcasing it under the cabinet's light, we left the comfort of the air-conditioned antiques mall for the blistering heat of the street, making our way slowly to the car.

I got the Buick's air-conditioning blasting on high, but didn't pull away from the curb.

"Mother?"

"Yes, dear?"

"What if our clock hands *had* been gold . . . before we

took it to Mr. Timmons? And what if Mrs. Vancamp's clock had been authentic, before she had him clean it?"

Mother was staring straight ahead. "Yes, dear . . . I'm thinking the same dire thoughts. And what if Connie Grimes hadn't been angry with Timmons about an overcharge, but something completely different?"

"Like plundering clock parts?"

"Plundering clock parts. Yes."

I pulled out into the street, and we drove home in silence. But our two little brains were buzzing.

A Trash 'n' Treasures Tip

Sometimes, a knock-off will be priced high, to help convince the buyer that it is real. If the owner suddenly gets cooperative and begins to reduce the price dramatically, the antique may be a fake. Unless the owner is trying to make bail, like Mother.

Chapter Seven

Don't Knock It

Senator Clark's campaign office was located in Pearl City Plaza—which wasn't really a plaza at all, rather the last block of Victorian buildings on Main Street. These grand old structures had been re-gentrified and transformed into bistros, boutiques, and specialty stores, giving downtown Serenity a much-needed boost.

Due to the senator's upcoming November midterm election, a team of young people had descended upon Serenity at the beginning of the summer, moving their operations into a storefront that had been abandoned by an antiques dealer who hadn't been able to compete with the nearby larger antiques mall where Mother and I had our booth.

Per Peggy Sue's arrangement, I had a late-morning appointment with the senator—I can't bring myself to write "my father," not yet anyway—and my first impulse had been to show up looking a slovenly mess (I'll let my therapist, Dr. Cynthia Hays tell me why, at my next appointment—if I think there's anything to it, I may share it with you).

But, since I was also meeting Tina for lunch afterward—and she was such a worrywart lately that if I had even one hair out of place, she might call 911—I fixed myself up and put on a leopard-print maternity sundress and gold gladiator sandals. (I guess we don't need Dr. Hays to interpret *that* choice of wardrobe.) (I think I'll also ask Dr. Hays about my compulsion to litter my writing with all these asides.)

Outside was gearing up to be another hot and humid August day, and I quickly exited my car parked on Main Street in front of the campaign office, then hustled through the slogan-plastered glass front door where an old air conditioner rattled and wheezed above the door, barely winning its campaign against the heat, greeting me by dripping water on my head.

The front room (there were others, trailing back in box-car fashion) also hummed noisily, as mostly young volunteers worked the phones at various desks and tables. This was a grass-roots effort, typical of the Midwest, nothing fancy: donated furniture, stained carpeting, scrounged amenities, poorly (and un-) paid staffers. Still, electricity sparked the air with the positive charge that only a campaign bullpen can generate.

A petite, pretty woman of about twenty, clipboard in hand, stepped forward to acknowledge me. She had a sorority girl look—long blond hair, tennis court tan, pink polo shirt and white slim skirt, a RE-ELECT EDWARD CLARK button pinned above one perky breast. Did the senator do his own job interviews for staffers?

"Hi," she chirped. "My name is Kara. Are you here to volunteer?"

"No," I said, businesslike. "I have an appointment to see Senator Clark."

"Oh." She sounded disappointed, probably hoping for another door-knocker willing to brave the heat. (Really? A pregnant woman with swollen ankles? In the world of volunteer politics, hope springs eternal, if not logical.) Kara crinkled her cute nose. "Would your name be Brandy?"

"It would."

A crisp nod. "Senator Clark said to expect you. Would you follow me, please?"

Kara turned, long hair swinging, leading me back to a second room where staffers worked at computers, then on through a break room with homemade goodies spread out on a table to keep up morale (though no one was nibbling at the moment), and finally to the caboose—a small, windowless room with an exit door to the alley.

Above the alley door, a newer air conditioner was noiselessly keeping the senator cool as he half-sat on the edge of a black metal desk, talking on his cell. He was wearing a crisply pressed white shirt—sleeves rolled—with a sky-blue silk tie, navy slacks, and mirror-shine shoes. From one wrist, an expensive-looking gold watch winked at us as we stood in doorway. I'd trade that Rolex in for a Timex before shaking any farmer hands, if I were him.

The senator, aware of our presence, quickly ended his conversation, slapped the high-end cell phone closed like Captain Kirk cutting Scotty off, and gestured for us to enter.

Kara, however, hung back, having completed her task of delivering me, then dutifully disappeared.

"Please sit," Senator Clark said, gesturing to one of two gray metal folding chairs in front of the desk.

As I did so, he retreated behind to a black padded swivel chair opposite.

Of course, I knew a bit about Senator Edward Clark, as he had represented our state for over twenty-five years, first as a state senator and then a United States senator. He was a widower, his wife having died some years ago of ovarian cancer. He had several grown children. He was a moderate, the kind of politician who was equally popular and unpopular with his own and the rival party, and passionate about Midwestern values—all of which made him hard to beat in an election year.

So *why* was he spending the August Senate recess in small-town Serenity, instead of in one of Iowa's bigger cities, or even just coasting on his popularity and fishing in Canada?

Because *this* time he was up against a formidable candidate, another moderate, a middle-aged woman with a large constituency; and sometimes Midwesterners can be fickle and want a change.

Iowans are a self-important breed when it comes to politics; they are accustomed to being the butts of derision as heartland hicks most of the time, but the attention that their early presidential primary casts upon the state provides a sense of self-importance even on off-year elections.

If appearances alone could guarantee a candidate's re-election, however, Senator Clark would win—the age lines in his chiseled face, the gray at the temples, only added to the man's movie-star sex appeal.

(*Yikes!* This is my *father* I'm talking about. Dr. Hays will have a *field day* with that!)

"I'm really glad you decided to come see me," he said, sounding genuine. But then, didn't *all* successful politicians?

He was saying, "Peggy Sue told me about the baby you're carrying. Brandy, I really admire you for that—what a selfless thing to do for a friend."

I shrugged. Then, alluding to my not-so-nice-behavior at our first meeting, I said, "I'm *not* a complete—" I was going to use the "s" word, but substituted another of Mother's favorites, the more socially acceptable "nincompoop."

"When is the baby due?" he asked.

"Two months." I shifted in the chair, which was almost

as uncomfortable on my bottom as this meeting was all over.

"You'd never know it."

"Senator," I said, and tried not to make it sound either hostile or pitiful, "I really don't know what you expect of me. . . ."

He raised his eyebrows. "I don't have any expectations. How about you? What do you expect of me?"

That blindsided me, but I guess it shouldn't have—I mean, it was so like a politician.

"Well, nothing," I said flatly. "It's a little late for anything, isn't it?"

"Is it?"

I didn't hide my annoyance as I said, "If you're going to answer every question with a question, I might as well concede defeat right now, Senator. Why did you tell my sister you wanted to see me? Or did she tell you *I* asked to see *you*? That would be just like her, trying to manipulate us both."

My little impromptu stump speech made an impression, I guess, because suddenly he sat forward. "Brandy, I did ask to see you. Wanted to talk to you. Because . . . I don't know anything about you. Hell, I didn't know you *existed* until very recently. If I *had*, I would have done the right thing."

"And we're back to the other day, in the alley. It's not nice, but I'll say it again, if I have to. By 'the right thing,' do you mean you'd have married Peggy Sue, or paid for her to get rid of me?"

The senator's tanned faced turned a little pale, his lips forming a thin line. Yet his response came quickly.

"Neither," he said. "Even though I wasn't married at the time, I also wasn't in love with Peggy Sue. And I believe I already told you I don't believe in abortion."

"Politicians have been known to flip-flop on that issue."
His smile was grim but patient. "Not me. You can check
my record on that one. . . . But I want you to believe that I
would have taken care of you both financially, over the
years, if I had known."

"Oh, I'm sure that's right . . ."

He sighed in relief. "Good."

". . . I'm sure you do want me to believe that."

His frown was so pained it almost hurt me to see it; almost. "Brandy, please . . ."

"You want me to let you off easy? No way, Senator.
Peggy Sue was very young and very impressionable and
very much in love with you."

Another sigh, but no relief in it at all. "Infatuated. There's
a difference."

"Not really! Not to a pregnant eighteen-year-old, anyway!" I sounded like an accusative child. Which I was.

Slowly, Senator Clark got out of his chair, came around
the desk, and stood looking down at me. "I did a stupid,
irresponsible thing," he admitted. "But I was young, too.
Not *as* young as Peggy Sue, not enough for that to be a
good excuse . . . but it . . . it was a lifetime ago."

"Yeah. Right. My lifetime."

He tried again. "Brandy, I *was* attracted to Peggy Sue.
And very fond of her. She was a beautiful young woman
and a big help to my campaign in those early days. I was
new at the political game, and not ready for how, as you
say, an impressionable young person can become emotionally vulnerable to someone he or she admires. And I didn't
understand how vulnerable *I* was, with my future on the
line as a public servant, and living so many, many lonely
nights on the road."

That would have been an easy speech to deride, but it
did seem sincere. Not politician sincere—*sincere*.

When I didn't say anything, he gave up yet another sigh

and went on, a man trudging through a swamp because there was no other route available to him.

"Brandy, I thought Peggy Sue had gone to Paris at the end of that summer—to study design. She had told me about her plans . . . which didn't include me. I'm not making an excuse for the affair—it's just that I thought we both had an understanding."

"You mean, that she'd go her way and you'd go yours."

He nodded. "Have you never had—it's a terrible word— a fling? A summer romance? A weak moment?"

I didn't answer, but my mind was filled with the memory of a certain high school class reunion. Yup, I had his DNA, all right.

"Brandy, why didn't she get in touch with me about the pregnancy? I'd have made every financial arrangement necessary for you and Peggy Sue to have a secure future. But she never contacted me. *Why?*"

"Embarrassment? Shame? Perhaps Peggy Sue felt you wouldn't *want* to marry her, and that if you did, you'd feel trapped. Maybe your career would be ruined. And you two would have a loveless tragedy of a marriage. Who can say?" I shrugged. "I'm not sure Peggy Sue knows why."

Denise Gardner appeared in the doorway, wearing a clinging purple silk dress and matching pair of high heels; the aide's dark almond-shaped eyes widened at my presence. Was that alarm? Had my father (*there—I typed it*) not cleared my visit with her?

"Senator, it's time for the luncheon with the Women's Political Action Committee," she told him. "Your car is waiting out back. . . ."

"Yes, yes, thank you, Denise. In a moment." He did not hide his irritation at this interruption.

The Dragon Lady retreated, and my host's attention returned to me. "I will say this for the late and apparently little lamented Connie Grimes—if it hadn't been for her, I might never have known about you. So for that much, I'm grateful."

I snorted, finding his words hard to swallow. "You're grateful for receiving an anonymous letter about an illegitimate child?"

The senator was heading to a metal coat tree to retrieve his suit jacket. "Actually," he said, "the letter wasn't anonymous."

"No?"

"The Grimes woman signed it and gave her full contact information. She said she knew about my 'love child,' and . . . she wanted money."

I nearly fell off my chair. Which wouldn't have been great for either me or the baby. *"What?"*

He nodded, unrolling his shirtsleeves, lifting an eyebrow. "I told Denise to tell Mrs. Grimes that I'd let the chips fall where they may."

I stood, before I *did* fall off the chair. "Then . . . you didn't pay her anything?"

"No. No hush money for her or anybody. The first rule of politics these days is that the cover-up is worse than the crime."

So now I was a *crime.* Anyway, for that to be the "first rule," a lot of politicians still seemed to be breaking it.

"And," he said, and slipped on the jacket, snugged his tie, tugged at his shirt cuffs, "I never heard from that unfortunate woman again. . . . How do I look?"

I couldn't help but smile. "Like a winning candidate."

"Is that a smile, Brandy?"

"It might be."

This time it was Kara who appeared in the entryway.

"Ready?" the blond staffer asked.

"As ready as I'm ever going to be," he said.

She approached him. "Should I make arrangements for dinner?"

He shook his head. "Too many contingencies this afternoon. Soon as I know, I'll call your cell."

The senator put a hand on her waist as she leaned forward and kissed him on the cheek. Then she flounced out of the room. Okay, maybe not flounced. But when a woman that good-looking exits a room, the flounce is implicit.

Meanwhile, my smile had wilted. As Mother would say, a tiger can never change its spots (telling her that should be "leopard" never does any good). And here I had been warming to the blaggard. (Since I was feeling like an orphan child out of Dickens, that's the word that occurred to me.)

Having withdrawn the smile, I gave him a smirk. "*Another* intern heading off to Paris after the summer?"

His smile wasn't *exactly* patronizing. "No, Kara baby-sits me with a firm hand . . ."

Some baby-sitter.

". . . because she's my youngest daughter."

I felt my face flush.

Then I asked, "Does she . . . know about me?"

"No. I thought I'd leave that to up to you." He smiled, seeming genuinely amused. "But I think you'd like each other—you have a lot in common. You both have a lot of gumption."

Now *he* was doing Dickens!

Then he exited the alley door, leaving me alone with my red face.

I walked into Allie's Tea Room, just down the street from the campaign office, at a few minutes to noon, beating Tina and managing to snag the last table-for-two at the popular eatery, where ladies loved to lunch and munch on speciality sandwiches, homemade soups, and wicked desserts.

A few brave souls were having their food out on a patio that faced the Mississippi, the blue water alive with diamond-like sparkles (it's not *always* muddy) under a high, bright sun. Me, I preferred to admire that aquatic vista from the coolness of the Great Indoors. Right now, a large white barge was passing slowly, its stomach stuffed with grain, making its winding way downriver to St. Louis or beyond. The last time I sat on the patio with Mother, she began singing, basso profundo, "Ole Man River," which she pronounced "ribber," claiming that was the Paul Robeson interpretation.

Come to think of it, maybe *that* was why I stopped eating out on the patio.

Speaking of stomachs, mine was growling. Where the heck was Tina? While we're waiting for my BFF, I'll tell you a little about the tea room.

Allie's was owned by Allie, natch, a lovely African-American woman in her early forties (I'm guessing) who had worked in the kitchen of what had been called just the Tea Room for a number of years. During a rough patch of business, the owner decided to shut the place down and retire. Allie stepped up and offered to buy him out and now, after a year, she was making a go of it in a tough business in a rough economy . . . so hats off to her!

Tina appeared, plopping down in the chair across from me. She looked adorable in a tropical floral spaghetti-strap sundress, her natural blonder-than-my-bottle-blond hair sleek and shiny as corn silk, makeup perfect, face glowing as if *she* were the expectant mother (or that could be the heat). A good thing she was my best friend, or I'd hate her.

"I couldn't find a parking place," she said, slightly out of breath. "I could've used your pal Red Feather."

Red Feather is my Indian spiritual guide, who (when respectfully summoned) can get me parking places. Honestly, I don't know how he does it. I can be stopped at a light, call upon Red Feather, and wish for a parking place . . . then up ahead someone will rush to their car, jump in, and pull out—often with a confused, under-a-spell expression.

As much as I appreciate a good parking spot, however, Red Feather isn't so hot at helping me avoid parking *tickets*. But we're working on that.

(P.S. I don't ask my Indian feather guide for money; that would be too selfish and greedy. But once, last winter, when I was in the shoe department of Ingram's department store, I did request a pair of UGG boots half-off, and suddenly there they were, in just my size. And UGGs *never* go on sale! Now do you believe in Indian spirit guides?)

A waitress came over and Tina and I ordered the same thing: curry tuna croissant, fruit, and iced tea. When our server had gone, Tina leaned forward intimately, as not to unduly entertain the sharp-eared ladies at neighboring tables.

"Well, give already," she said. "How did it go with Daddy?"

Of course, I had told her that I was meeting with the senator, as we never keep anything from each other. Well . . . practically never. There was one time, though, way back when, when I went out once with this guy she liked, behind her back, but all he did was talk about Tina. (Sorry, honey.)

(This is Tina speaking. I just read the advance proof pages, and called Brandy's very nice and accommodating editor, who said there was time enough for me to respond before this book went to press. Brandy, I knew about that date . . . and I forgave you. Besides, I'd already had my eye on Kevin.)

(Brandy speaking. NOTE TO SELF: never let anybody read advance proof pages again!)

"I'm not to going to tell you a thing," I said, "unless you promise not to refer to the man as my 'Daddy.' "

"Well, that's a step up, anyway."

"What is?"

"You referred to him as '*the* man,' not '*that* man.' Progress. Baby steps."

Everything was "baby" with her at the moment.

Our curry tuna croissants arrived, and between bites, Tina tried again. "Sooooo . . . tell me all about it!"

What the hey. I did, even mentioning how Connie Grimes had tried to blackmail the senator. For money.

Tina's tuna croissant tumbled from her hand. "Oh, my lord—that woman must have been out of her mind."

"You're thinking of Mother," I said. "Connie wasn't crazy, just evil." I paused, to see if lightning would strike me for defaming the dead, then went on. "Evil, and desperate for money."

Tina shrugged. "I don't know why she would be. Her husband has a good job, doesn't he? And they have a nice enough house. I mean, how much more does a person need?"

I said, "Plenty, if she's trying to keep up with Peggy Sue Hastings."

"Good point." Tina frowned. "What if Connie was trying to feather her nest for *herself*? Haven't you heard the rumors about her husband and that secretary where he works?"

I nodded. Gossip held no appeal to me, but Mother was Rumor Central in Serenity. So I knew much more than I wanted to about all kinds of people, many of whom I'd never met.

Tina sighed. "Blackmailing a senator was *some* risk to take—I mean, the woman could've gone to jail."

"If she hadn't been killed first."

Tina pushed her plate forward, leaned in, elbows on the table, hands tented. "So what does your boyfriend the chiefie have to say? Where are the local fuzz in the investigation? Do they have a suspect yet?"

"Not that I know of. Somehow I don't expect phone call updates from Tony on this matter."

"What about your mother? *Vivian,* I mean, not Peggy Sue."

"Please . . ."

"Does Viv have a suspect in mind? I mean, she must have *some* inkling."

I stared at Tina. Talking about Connie's murder was the last thing I expected from her, knowing how she felt about me being any further involved in so stressful a pursuit as an unofficial murder inquiry, during the last trimester of the pregnancy.

Was she fishing around to see if I'd kept my word?

Guardedly, I said, "Look, I'm not actively investigating or anything . . . but I'm also not discouraging Mother from doing so."

"Really? Why not?"

"Because rubber-stamping her sleuthing is how I got her back on her medication."

Tina's response wasn't exactly short, but close to it. "Yes, I know . . . you already explained that. I'm not being critical, Brandy, I just wanted to know if there was a suspect, that's all. No biggie."

I knew my friend well; maybe better than she did herself . . . and somehow her interest in the case *was* a "biggie." I just didn't know why.

I decided to throw her a bone. "Well, this is hardly worth mentioning, but Mother met a woman in jail who had been ransacking the house across the street from Connie's the morning she was killed, and—"

"Surely," Tina cut in, with uncharacteristic rudeness, "the police have already questioned this home invader about what she saw."

"Yes . . . but the thief can't remember much."

"So?"

"So Mother has this harebrained idea"—I had to stop and laugh—"to have her jailhouse friend put under hypnosis."

But Tina didn't laugh. Tina just stared.

Suddenly—and I promised earlier that I wouldn't do this to you, but facts are facts—I had to pee really bad because of my condition.

So I left the table, saying, "Order me one of those gooey chocolate brownies, would you?"

I scurried off to the ladies' room, a one-stall affair, thankfully not busy. I had finished washing my hands and was opening the door, when a woman barged in, pushed me back, then locked us in.

"Really?" I said. "In a bathroom? How classy is that?"

Top aide Denise was standing there, in these close quarters, pointing a red nail-polished finger at me. "I want you to *stop* bothering Senator Clark!"

I put hands on hips. Supergirl. Super-preggers-girl, anyway. "I wasn't *bothering* him—*he* invited me to his office . . . or didn't he share that with you?"

Judging by her surprised expression, my assumption that the boss hadn't bothered clearing our meeting with his top aide was correct.

She lowered the pointing finger, as if reluctantly holstering a gun, but her threatening manner remained.

"If the press gets wind of your relationship," she said through white little teeth, "Senator Clark may very well lose the election in November . . . and I've worked too hard to let that happen!"

Not *"we've,"* but *"I've"* worked too hard.

I smirked. "And *you'd* be out of a job, with a career path to the White House blocked. Boo freakin' hoo."

"Just *stay* away from him!"

"Or what?"

I might end up like Connie Grimes?

"Or . . . you'll be sorry."

Lame.

"Just tell me," she said, and it seemed like she was about to cry, "is it really *his?*"

And her eyes went to my tummy.

Was *that* the relationship she suspected?

Obviously it was; only, I hadn't figured it, seeing the senatorial situation only from my own warped end of the telescope.

I was so flustered, I couldn't speak. She unlocked the bathroom door, threw me a look of daggers, and left.

Brazen as I'd sounded, my knees felt weak, my legs were trembling. Was it possible that über-aide Denise, in her protective zeal, had been the one to silence Connie? If so, what else might the Dragon Lady be capable of?

I shook my head. Maybe I'd been reading too many political thrillers lately. Still—I looked down at my protruding stomach—was I prepared to jeopardize two lives over this increasingly convoluted ordeal?

I left the bathroom, returning to Tina at the table.

"You won't believe what just happened," I said, sitting down.

My friend looked wan.

"What's the matter?" I asked. "Don't you feel well?"

After a long moment she said, "Brandy, I'm sorry, but . . . I just have to tell you something. . . ."

"What is it, sweetie?"

Then she dropped a bombshell.

"You need to know that I . . . honey, I went to see Connie the morning she was murdered."

138   *Barbara Allan*

A Trash 'n' Treasures Tip

To help authenticate an antique, look for the maker's signature: a brand or paper label on furniture, a name or initial on pottery, or an identifying mark stamped on glass, ceramics or metal. Mother once thought she had bought a signed painting by Grandma Moses at a flea market until she got home, put on her reading glasses, and on closer inspection read, "To Grandma, love Moses."

Chapter Eight

Knock On Wood

Allie's Tea Room had cleared out enough for Tina and me to have some privacy at our table-for-two. And when I'd recovered from my friend's admission that she, too, had been at Connie Grimes's house the morning of the murder, I asked, "Why on earth would *you* go?"

Tina swallowed. I could even hear the *gulp*. "To ask her—to *beg* her—to stop harassing you. I . . . I was afraid the stress might hurt the . . . the . . ." She choked on the last of it, never getting "baby" out, eyes tearing.

I reached for her hand resting on the table, giving it a squeeze. "*Nothing's* going to hurt the baby, Tina. You needn't have gone. I'm fine. *We're* fine."

Or was I / were we? Having been on Prozac since I moved home—the only way I could live with Mother—and now anti-depressant free for seven months, I was beginning to see cracks in the veneer of my own tender psyche.

But I wasn't about to let Tina see them.

"Tell me what happened," I said gently. "Did you see Connie? Talk to her?"

Tina shook her head. "I rang the bell, again and again,

but she didn't answer, so . . ." She shrugged. "I just tucked my tail between my legs and left."

"Well, it's a good thing you didn't go inside. That would certainly have complicated things."

"She must have already been"—Tina gave an involuntary shiver—"dead."

"Or just didn't want to answer. At any rate, there's no need for you to come forward with this information."

Her eyes jumped with relief. "You think so?"

Now I shrugged. "What do you know that would help the investigation? I mean, you don't know anything, do you?"

"How could I?"

"Did you see something, someone—someone else leaving, maybe? Or a car you passed coming or going?"

Tina's brow furrowed momentarily, then she said, "Well . . . after I pulled out of Hidden Pines, I *did* notice a blue SUV in my rearview mirror, coming from the other direction. But I can't say for sure that it turned in at the Pines."

Could it be the same van Mother saw leaving the housing development some time later? Or just one of hundreds zipping around the streets of Serenity?

"I don't mean to sound like a cop," I said, "but what about the make of the car?"

Like, was it a Cadillac Escalade? But I didn't want to lead the witness. . . .

"I didn't notice. I'm kind of dumb about that kind of thing. If Kevin had seen it, *he'd* know." She shrugged again. "Just a blue SUV. Light blue. Pretty new. Clean."

I nodded, then reiterated that she should remain mum on her trip to see Connie, unless directly asked by someone in law enforcement.

Still, my friend seemed understandably troubled. She asked, "What about your mother's plan to put that jailhouse acquaintance of hers under hypnosis? Robbing the house across the way, *she* might remember me."

I shook my head. "I can't see this hypnosis thing happening. Tony won't ever agree to it. It's just another one of Mother's crazy, rattle-brained ideas that I'm pretending to go along with, to keep her happy . . . and happily medicated."

We fell silent. I wondered if Tina was thinking the same thing I was: that all too many of Mother's rattle-brained ideas had come to fruition. . . .

Finally Tina sighed and smiled in resignation. "Okay, then . . . I won't worry about it. . . ."

I smiled. "Why waste the energy? Besides, if that jailbird *does* remember you, she'll only corroborate that you rang the doorbell, then left. Right?"

"Hadn't thought of it that way."

"You just didn't read as much Nancy Drew as I did. Enough said on the subject. Now, how about getting down to serious concerns? Like splitting one of those brownies?"

On my drive home, the Buick's air conditioner conked out, which was frustrating in a "What *now?*" sort of way; but did give me the perfect opportunity to follow up a lead on my own.

The morning of the murder, the police couldn't locate Connie's husband at the car dealership where he worked. If he wasn't there, where *was* he?

Fred—or Freddie, as Connie always called him—reportedly made a comfortable living selling high-end cars on commission. Comfortable, at least, before a sagging economy inspired folks to either hold on to their cars longer, or buy cheaper models, or even trade in for used ones.

The luxury car dealership, located at the mouth of the notoriously treacherous bypass, was much smaller than others in Serenity, a fact emphasized by the current lack of inventory in the lot.

Under the pretense of needing a new car, I slowly cruised the rows of BMWs, Mercedes, and Caddies, looking for blue models that might fit the description of the SUV seen in the vicinity of Hidden Pines.

Seemed to me that Fred Grimes had a unique opportunity to get behind the wheel of a car off this lot, drive home, dispatch his wife, then return the car here, where it could remain hidden in plain sight.

That's right—all that Nancy Drew I bragged about to Tina had really paid off. . . .

I pulled up to a powder-blue Escalade—exactly like Peggy Sue's—turned off the Buick, and got out. I walked around the big-sticker vehicle, then peered in the windows. To a bystander, I might appear just another prospective buyer (if an unlikely one, based upon the battered Buick I'd arrived in), and not a shrewd female sleuth.

Did I say "shrewd?" What did I expect to find, anyway? A bloody footprint on the driver's side?

"May I help you?" a male voice asked. Friendly enough, if touched with skepticism. He'd apparently noted the Buick.

I turned to see Fred Grimes in white shirt-sleeves, red tie, and navy slacks. Early fifties, a tad overweight, with a drinker's nose, and a fairly convincing comb-over, Fred had left his glory days behind at high school, mostly on the football field, where then-slender cheerleader Connie must have thought he'd be quite the catch. What she caught, according to Peggy Sue, had been years of disappointment and discontent.

"Oh," he said flatly, "it's you," his friendly, hoping-for-a-sale expression fading.

"Yes . . . uh . . . hi, Mr. Grimes."

" 'Fred' is all right, Brandy."

"Okay, Fred. I'm kind of surprised to see you back at work."

"My first day. We missed you at the funeral."

"I didn't think I'd be welcome, frankly."

Fred didn't contradict that notion.

(We hadn't sent flowers, either. Or a card. At the Hallmark Store, they were fresh out of *So sorry my dog and I found your loved one's body stabbed with a kitchen knife in your living room*.)

Finally he said, "So can I help you?"

"Would you believe I need a new car? I sure like the looks of this baby." I gestured to the Caddy.

Fred's eyes narrowed skeptically. "That right?" he said blandly.

I'd come this far. Blurting my ridiculous interest in a Cadillac seemed to be the story I was stuck with, so I put on my sincerest face. "Yes, I've just come into some money—a final settlement from my ex."

His eyes remained narrow and suspicious. "Really. I believe I sold your sister an Escalade just like that."

I gave him a mischievous smile. "Boy, it would really get her goat if I got one like hers."

Fred grunted. "Heard all kinds of reasons for buying a car—that's a first."

"Peg and me, we don't exactly get along."

"I've heard."

From Connie, no doubt.

"Really just a friendly rivalry," I said lamely.

He clearly didn't care either way. In fact, his body language indicated he was about to turn and let me browse on my own.

So I blurted again. This time it was: "How about a test drive?"

He studied me a moment, weighing the possible waste of his time. "In this Cadillac?"

"Absolutely." I was chipper as all heck. Making myself sick. "My ex's money is burnin' a hole in my pocketbook."

But then he shrugged. "Why not." He didn't have enough energy to make a question out of it. "Not like we're busy."

Fred excused himself, walked over and into a rectangular building distinguished only by the famous automotive logos in its showroom windows, then returned a few minutes later with the keys.

I climbed in behind the wheel, adjusted the seat, fixed the belt comfortably around my baby bulge, turned the car on, and got the air conditioner going full blast—the *other* hidden agenda of this visit.

Fred, in the passenger seat, said, "If you take Tipton Road out of town, you can judge for yourself how smooth the ride is."

The asphalt highway was notorious for cracks and potholes, and in my delicate condition I wasn't sure such a route was wise; but this had been my idea, hadn't it? So I steered the Escalade across the bypass and took the turnoff.

I hit a few potholes on purpose, barely feeling the bumps.

"This *is* a nice ride," I agreed. Then said, "Fred, I know this is awkward for you. Connie and I were not exactly friends, but I really am sorry for your loss."

He took a moment to answer. "You're not sorry."

That was cold.

He gave a rumpled sideways smile that ranked with the worst smiles I ever saw. "And you know what else? I'm not sorry either."

You've probably noticed by now that I don't shock easily. But Fred's frankness left me speechless.

"Not happy she was *killed*," he amended, "but not sorry she's gone. I don't like thinking she spent her last moments in pain . . . and fear . . ."

He touched the thumb and middle finger of his right hand to the bridge of his nose, momentarily.

Then he went on. "And don't think I didn't love her once . . . but we haven't had a marriage for quite some time. She was a lovely young woman but grew into an unpleasant envious one—did you know that neither of our boys flew home for her funeral? Her own sons."

My eyes were getting damp now. Not for her. For him.

His big shoulders shrugged. "For a lot of years, she went her way, and I went mine. We even kept separate bank accounts—along with bedrooms. . . . Does that cover everything you wanted to know, Brandy?"

Obviously, he was no dope. But *I* was feeling like one. I slowed the car, pulling it onto the shoulder, then, leaving it idling, looked at him. "Yes, Fred, you covered a lot of it. Could I ask you about a couple of other things?"

His grin was sudden. "Drove her crazy, you know, you and your mother, lately. Getting in the papers all the time playing *Murder She Wrote*. She hated that almost as much as she envied that sister of yours. . . . Go ahead, Brandy. Ask."

"Okay, no easy way to ask this, Fred, but . . . I'd like to know why the police couldn't find you the morning she was murdered."

His eyes widened and he grinned again, bigger but not as awful; this was just amusement. Utter amusement. "Oh! *I* get it! You're wondering if I stuck that knife in her. Sorry to disappoint you, sweetie. I didn't. Anything else I can do for you? Wanna test-drive a Mercedes or anything?"

"Where *were* you?"

Fred turned his face to the windshield, contemplating whether or not to answer. Then he shrugged. "You'll figure it out anyway, because we're gonna get married soon."

"Married?"

"Yeah." He nodded toward my tummy. "You seem familiar with the birds and the bees. I was with my girlfriend, at *her* place."

Some alibi. About as good as the one Fred MacMurray had in *Double Indemnity*.

"Now, turn this car around," he growled, "and stop wasting my time. If I'm on the lot, I might even sell a damn car today. Stranger things have happened."

I arrived home, sweaty and crabby. Although the house was cool inside, it apparently wasn't cold enough for my furball friend, who for once did not greet me dancing at the door, wanting to play. Instead I found her in the kitchen, on her tummy, spread-eagled on the cool tile floor.

Mother flew in from the dining room.

"It's about *time* you got home!" she said, eyes wild behind the glasses. She was wearing the blue cotton housedress she reserved only for the hottest of days. "We haven't a moment to lose! Chief Cassato has agreed to see me, and we *must* go before he changes his mind."

Or came to his senses. . . .

I groaned. "Please tell me this doesn't have anything to do with hypnosis."

"Look into my eyes! It has *everything* to do with hypnosis, dear. I've already spoken to Tilda, and she is ready, willing, and able to put Rhonda under her spell."

For the uninitiated, meet Matilda "Tilda" Tompkins—New Age guru, part-time hypnotist, and full-time kook. She lived in a dilapidated house opposite the cemetery, rooming with a dozen cats, all (she claims) reincarnations of souls dead and buried across the way. Any questions?

"Mother," I said, straining for patience, "you'll just be wasting the chief's time."

"No, dear, *you're* wasting *our* time. Now chop chop!" And she brushed by me, heading out the door to the car.

There was no dissuading Mother once she had that determined look on her face. And hadn't I promised to take her wherever she wanted to go, if she took her medication? A deal was a deal.

I did find solace in the fact that at least I'd get to see Tony. We hadn't had a chance to spend any time together since Sushi and I stumbled onto the late Connie Grimes.

The modern redbrick building of the dual police station/fire department was located next to the jail, kitty-corner from the courthouse. As per Mother's instructions, I parked in a handicapped spot near the front entrance, hanging the required tag from the rearview mirror.

(Mother had gotten the tag years ago when she had surgery for an ingrown toenail, and continues to make use of it, even though I have consistently warned her that she will spend an eternity driving around Hell, looking for a parking place.)

We entered the station, then walked through the utilitarian waiting area and up to the female dispatcher, sequestered behind the bullet-proof (but, unfortunately, not Mother-proof) glass.

The middle-aged, brown-haired, bespectacled woman, whose name tag said DIANE, glanced up from her monitor. Mother leaned in to the microphone embedded in the glass, announcing herself using the painfully artificial British aristocrat accent she reserved to impress peons. "Vivian Borne to see the chief at *his* invitation."

Diane just looked at her.

Mother continued. "The chief and I have vital business to conduct, so your prompt attention would be *most* appreciated."

I had learned that in moments like this, I could do one of two things: (a) retreat a few steps behind Mother's back and make "crazy" circles with my finger at my head, or (b) pretend nothing was wrong, taking a perverse pleasure in watching Mother's victim squirm.

I usually chose "b." Quality entertainment comes no cheaper.

But the dispatcher did not squirm; neither did she smirk at Mother's behavior, merely saying in a businesslike manner, "I'll buzz you on in, Mrs. Borne."

"*Thank* you, my dear," said Lady Vivian Borne. Then to me, her accent suddenly gone, she whispered, "I think Diane is on the brink of cultivation."

Here's what Mother meant: once she had found a dispatcher's weakness—which could be anything from a desire for a part in Mother's next play to an autographed glossy of George Clooney (secretly signed by Mother, of course)—Mother would have an "in" at the police station. Since the previous, Mother-cultivated dispatcher had been dispatched to another assignment (precisely for helping her), Vivian Borne was in need of a new mole.

We moved through a steel-plated door—Mother in the lead—into the inner-station sanctum, then down a long beige-tiled corridor whose tedium was broken by walls lined with group photos of policemen of bygone days. Somehow I always felt they were looking at us in an accusatory fashion, but Mother never seemed to notice.

As we went by the interview room, where only a short time ago Mother had been languishing on a murder charge, she gave it not a glance, marching on ahead of me as if she were the chief herself or maybe the mayor.

The office of the actual chief was the last door on the

left (didn't that sound ominous?), and Mother beat me there, sailing on in—it stood open. As I trailed after, she was already plopping down in the nearest of two chairs opposite the chief seated at his desk.

Tony, in a starched light blue shirt and navy tie, gave me the briefest of smiles before reverting to his standard expressionless mask.

Mother chirped ridiculously, "You wanted to see me, Chief?" Fortunately, the British accent was gone; but now she sounded jaunty, like Jean Arthur in a Frank Capra movie or maybe Lois Lane on the old *Superman* show.

I rolled my eyes. Do you think if a person rolls her eyes too much that they eventually might just fall out? And bounce away like little rubber balls? I was starting to wonder.

Tony was saying with admirable patience, "I believe *you* asked to see *me*, Vivian. Well, here we are."

"Yes! Here we are. Together again."

Perhaps Tony had a similar concern for his eyes, because he managed not to roll them. "Please make it brief. I'm busy."

Mother waved one hand. "Well, *of course* you are! Do you think I don't understand the grave responsibilities you face? The pressures and demands of your high office? Would I waste your time just to come in and babble on and on and on, like The Madwoman of Chaillot? No. I will be succinct."

Bouncy bouncy. Bouncy bouncy.

She was settling into the chair like she might stay a while. "As you'll recall, I was recently in the hoosegow . . ."

Tony closed his eyes.

". . . and while I was serving my time, I had the pleasure of making the acquaintance of a charming young woman named Rhonda."

"Yes," Tony snapped, "I'm well aware of Rhonda."

So much for patience.

He was saying, "We've questioned her in relation to the Connie Grimes investigation. And she could give us no pertinent information. Is that all, Vivian?"

I asked, "Was Rhonda cooperative?"

Tony nodded. "I believe she understood that helping us might benefit her when it comes time for sentencing. But I'm afraid she couldn't come up with anything useful."

Mother raised a finger. "Ah . . . but I believe she still *can*."

She made him wait for it.

With perhaps a hint of Brit, she intoned, "*I* have been doing some research on the Internet . . ."

Oh, no, I thought. *Not* the Internet, where anyone can make a case for anything, true or false. Not the fine folks at Wikipedia again!

Mother went on. "I feel quite certain that if Rhonda is put under hypnosis, she will remember who came and went from the Grimes habitat the morning of the murder. She may have seen a good deal, while holed up with her loot in the house across the street." She pressed on before Tony's open mouth could produce a word. "I would assume you have heard of Serenity's own Matilda Tompkins, and her amazing powers of hypnosis?"

Tony's eyebrows shot up. Who in town didn't know about the crazy cat guru? His mouth remained open. And wordless.

"Well," Mother said, with the sly smile of Perry Mason just as the final clue came to him and the culprit was about to be unmasked in the courtroom, "Tilda has agreed— with your *permission,* of course—to hypnotize Rhonda." She cackled. Yes, cackled. "You would be astonished by the secrets we all have running rampant in our subconsciousness." That didn't sound quite right to her, and she added, ". . . es."

Tony sat forward slowly, eyes glued to Mother. "In certain cases, Vivian, I don't think I'd be 'astonished' in the least."

I almost giggled. But we were in a police station, after all.

"Then you agree we should put Rhonda with Tilda," Mother said, a statement not a question.

I sat forward. This would be a new record for the chief—shutting down Mother's latest wild scheme in five minutes flat. . . .

But Tony said, "Yes, Vivian. I agree. But *I'll* make the arrangements."

"Excellent!"

"And *you* are not to be present during the hypnosis."

Mother sat forward, alarmed. "By 'present,' do you mean, in the room during the process?"

"No. I mean on the premises."

Mother scoffed, "Surely I can be in the *outer* room."

"No."

"How about on the porch?"

Tony shook his head.

"In the front yard?"

"No! And not in the backyard, either. You will be at *home,* Vivian, minding your own business, and out of our hair."

Mother looked crestfallen.

I said, "What if I promise to keep Mother under control in the outer room? After all, it's because of *her* that both Matilda and Rhonda have already agreed to the session. You take Mother entirely out of the equation, and who's to say whether these women will even want to cooperate with the police?"

Tony studied me for a moment. Could I be trusted?

Well, could I?

The sigh must have started down around the toes of his Florsheims. "All right, Brandy." He pointed a finger like a gun at Mother. "But no shenanigans."

She had a loony smile on her mug as she crossed her heart.

He frowned at her. "And don't think you'll be getting any information out of that cat-happy hypnotist, either. She'll be asked to leave the room once Rhonda has been put under, and instructed to answer our questions."

Mother acted hurt. "Why, I wouldn't do anything so unethical as to pry sensitive information out of Tilda . . . and Chief, a word of advice—you may not want to disparage the woman's cats. Who knows? You may be buried across the way yourself someday, and might wind up wanting a saucer of milk."

"Very funny," Tony grunted.

Mother glanced at me. She hadn't been joking.

Tony stood, thanked us for coming, and ushered us out into the hall. Mother marched victoriously on ahead, but Tony took my arm, gently.

"I'd like to see you tonight," he half whispered.

I smiled. "Thought you'd never ask."

"Pick you up at seven?"

"I'll wear my dancing shoes."

But of course, we wouldn't go dancing, or anywhere else the public could cast its disapproving eye on Serenity's Top Cop, out with a divorced woman (pregnant at that) and at least fifteen years younger than him.

Instead we would go to his secluded cabin, fix dinner together, and cuddle by the fire. What more could a girl want? (A sane mother, maybe?)

By midafternoon, Tony had arranged for Rhonda to be released into police custody, with the hypnosis set to take place in Matilda's home at four o'clock. Of course,

Mother insisted we be there an hour beforehand (Mother trusted Tony even less than he trusted her).

The house across from the cemetery was the kind of white two-story clapboard that people nowadays call shabby chic, but with an emphasis on the shabby. And, in Tilda's case, the tabby.

The hypnotist was one of Mother's hundreds of "very close friends," a list you got on via your willingness to put up with her. As I pulled our currently air-conditioning-free car up to the curb, our hostess was waiting in the shade of the weathered porch, seated in a white, paint-peeling wicker rocking chair.

Tilda was pushing fifty but could easily pass for forty with her slender figure, long golden red hair, and translucent skin, usually sans make-up, youthful freckles scattered carelessly across the bridge of her nose. She was wearing her standard Bohemian attire—plaid madras long full skirt, white peasant blouse, and Birkenstock sandals.

As Mother and I approached, Tilda stood and displayed an obviously anxious expression.

"Why, Tilda," Mother said, "you're looking lovely as ever."

"Thank you, Vivian," the woman said. "Come inside, out of the heat."

Soon we were in a small living room that had been transformed into a mystic shrine of soothing candles, healing crystals, and swirling mobiles of planet and stars—all for sale, as this was also her shop. Incense scent tinged the air, and from somewhere drifted the tinkling electronic sound of New Age music.

At the moment, only five cats were at large, lounging on the couch, recliner, and an oak rocker, over to which Tilda went, making a shooing motion.

"Scat, Eugene Lyle Wilkenson!" she commanded. "Make room for Brandy."

The yellow tabby regarded Tilda with bored eyes, then jumped down, and I took its place.

I had kind of a hard time believing this particular cat—which showed up as a kitten on Tilda's porch the day after Mr. Wilkenson's funeral—was the incarnation of the man, who had owned a dog kennel. If so, the dog lover must have had some bad karma to wind up a kitty.

(*NOTE TO SELF: do not be buried across the street from Tilda Tompkins.*)

Mother said to me, as if I were another of the cats, "Now, stay put, Brandy—Tilda and I have some business to attend to in the hypnosis suite."

I stopped rocking. "*Mother!* Remember what the chief said? No shenanigans! You agreed."

Mother laughed once. "My dear, I don't remember agreeing to any such thing. Perhaps *you* agreed, but *I* didn't. And in any case, Webster defines a shenanigan as 'a devious trick used especially for an underhand purpose,' and nothing I have in mind would *begin* to so qualify."

How many times had I been caught in Mother's web over such technicalities?

I pointed a warning finger. "Fine! But if you get into trouble, I won't help you get out of it!"

Mother smiled sweetly. "In the unlikely event that I should 'get into trouble,' I of course know that I can always depend upon you, my dear, for your aid and assistance."

And Mother took Tilda by the elbow, as if showing a guest to a church pew at a wedding, leading the hypnotist helpfully off to her own hypnosis room.

When is that medication going to kick in, anyway?

Fuming, I rocked faster, wondering what Mother had promised Matilda for her part in the conspiracy. What were they up to? Should I sneak in there and find out?

Thinking about Tony, I decided that the less I knew the better. Better a victim in this than an accomplice.

After only a few minutes, the two ladies returned. Tilda was in the process of shooing several other cats off the floral cat-hair-covered couch so the two women could sit, when Mother gasped.

She was staring out the front window. "They're *here* already!" Eyes and nostrils flaring, Mother turned to Tilda. "Didn't I tell you that that Tony Cassato can simply *not* be trusted? Thank goodness *we* came early!"

I stood and crossed to the window, also registering surprise. Not because the police car arrived ahead of schedule—I had expected that—but because it wasn't Tony exiting the vehicle.

The officer in charge, and now opening the back door for Rhonda, was Brian Lawson.

Mother said, "Oh, Brandy! Look! How nice—it's your old boyfriend."

Where was *Tony?* Why had he entrusted the session to someone else? Brian was certainly competent enough, under normal circumstances, just no match for Mother.

Rhonda, in her orange prison garb, hands shackled behind her, was escorted up the walk. Her brown hair stringy, she had a smug look going, and I wondered if once she got inside, the prisoner might have a change of mind and not go through with the hypnosis. Or make a break for it or something. . . .

Tilda opened the front door, and Brian—hand on the arm of his charge—stepped through with Rhonda.

Mother said cheerfully, "Ah, Officer Lawson—how nice to see that *you* will be handling the session. You have a much lighter, more compassionate touch than your chief."

The prisoner gave the young officer a sideways smirk.

"And how thoughtful it was of you to help me, Rhonda."

Now Mother was doing the Beach Boys. . . .

Brian's puppy-dog brown eyes went to me and—perhaps because of my quizzical expression—he offered, "The chief had a problem at the station and couldn't be here."

But he gave no details.

"Oh, that's unfortunate," Mother said disingenuously. "For all his faults, he is a *very* experienced officer." Her eyes went to Rhonda. "My, you're looking well, my dear. Have you lost some weight? The Pilates balls must be working."

"It ain't the balls," she snapped. "It's the lousy food!"

"Yes, it *was* terrible . . ."

"That's not what I mean, Viv! Thanks to *you* stickin' your nose in, now all we get is healthy stuff. Ugh!"

"You'll come to thank me for it, dear," Mother said, adding, "and again I'd like to thank you for agreeing to a mind-probe session."

"Ain't doin' it for *you*, Viv," Rhonda said with a sneer. "Doin' it for *me*." Her angry eyes looked at Brian. "I better get a reduced sentence, if I give you guys good info."

Patiently Brian said, "You've been told, Rhonda, we can't promise anything. But the judge will be informed of your cooperation."

The sneer vanished, her expression almost pleading. "Come on, it's gotta look really good on my record, right? Small change like me helping catch a killer? That's gotta be worth *something*."

Brian's voice turned gentle. "Rhonda, you cooperate today, I will personally put a good word in."

The woman sighed. "All right, then—let's *do* it. . . ."

Tilda, silent until now, spoke in a firm, businesslike manner. "How shall we proceed, Officer?"

"Well, first," Brian said lightly, "I need your permission

to inspect the hypnosis room, to make sure that there's nothing in there that might compromise the session."

I glanced at Mother, who wore her most angelic face.

Tilda seemed a little apprehensive, but compliant, saying, "I'm all right with that, Officer. The suite's just off the kitchen. Shall I take you there?"

"I'll find my way, thank you."

Leaving Rhonda with us, Brian disappeared into the back. I returned to the rocker while Mother and Tilda sat on the couch, a couple of cats materializing to curl up at their feet. Rhonda, preferring to stand, seemed to notice the decor for the first time, her eyes flitting over the New Age trappings.

Several minutes passed in silence, before Rhonda said, "What kind of crap is this, anyway?"

Tilda sat forward, poised to defend her lifestyle to her shackled guest, when Brian came back in, moving quickly to an abrupt halt.

In one hand was a small tape recorder, which he held up accusingly.

Mother's face turned crimson, and she stuttered, "Oh, my, how . . . however did *that* get in there?"

"However indeed?" Brian said dryly. He crossed to the couch, tossed the recorder between Mother and Tilda. "Yours I presume?"

Mother's expression turned sheepish. "Yes, I'm afraid it is. Well! You can't blame a girl for trying! Brian, I don't have to tell you how much the police have benefitted from my, and Brandy's, sleuthing efforts. Your chief is cutting his own throat, keeping me out of the loop!"

"*Is* he?"

Her expression now became contrite. "Please don't blame Tilda for this, or Brandy—they were both blissfully unaware of the little gizmo's presence."

Well, I had been, anyway. But I wouldn't say "blissfully."

Brian straightened and let out a deep sigh. "All right, then. I think we're ready for the session." And he proceeded to set the ground rules.

Mother and I were to remain in the New Age shrine/shop, while Brian, Matilda, and Rhonda would be sequestered in the hypnosis suite. Once Rhonda had been hypnotized and instructed to answer Brian's questions—restricted to who and what she had seen the morning of the murder—Tilda was to leave the room, reentering only when summoned by Brian, to bring Rhonda out of her trance.

During the session I spent my time (a) chiding Mother about her failed espionage attempt, (b) petting the cats, and then (c) ignoring those cats because my eyes began to itch.

After about half an hour, Brian called out to Tilda—who had spent her time dusting the many sale items in her living room—and she set down her duster and scurried off.

In another few minutes, Brian appeared with the handcuffed Rhonda, Tilda bringing up the rear.

Mother jumped up from the couch. "Well, how did it go? Was my suggestion a success?"

As if Brian would actually tell her.

"Fine," he said pleasantly. "But that's *all* you get, Vivian."

Mother guffawed. "Well, yes, certainly! It's not as if I were trying to pry any information out of you, Officer Lawson. I am merely an interested member of the public."

"Right," Brian said.

Behind the thick lenses, Mother's tiny magnified eyes bore in on Rhonda.

The woman shrugged. "Don't ask me, Viv—I don't remember nothing . . . but funny thing is, I feel like I had a good rest, and yet I'm sleepy at the same time. Weird, huh?" She yawned loudly, then turned to Brian. "Can we go? I want that butterscotch Dilly Bar from the Dairy Queen you promised me." Her eyes flashed accusingly Mother's way. "We don't get anything good like that in jail anymore."

I said, "We better go too, Mother." The sooner this afternoon came to an end, the better I liked it. Besides, I needed some time to get ready for my date tonight with Tony.

"Very well, dear," Mother said, picking up her purse from the floor by the couch. "But first, I need a glass of water—why, I'm so dry I could spit cotton! Tilda, I'll get it myself."

Outside, the car had turned into an oven even with the windows rolled down.

"Well, that sure was a waste of our time," I grumbled, climbing behind the wheel.

Next to me, Mother in mock innocence said, "*Was* it, dear?"

I twisted toward her. "*Wasn't* it?"

"I shouldn't think so! I have the whole session on tape."

"But Brian found the recorder!"

"He found the decoy—the one I *wanted* to be found—not the *other* one, more carefully concealed."

Which she must have retrieved when getting the glass of water.

I groaned, "Oh, Mother! You're going to get us into *so much* trouble!"

Her brow furrowed and she rested a thoughtful finger against one cheek. "In a way, dear, it's a pity that you ever broke up with that nice young Brian Lawson—such a nice young man, handsome . . . and putty in my hands. Chief Cassato makes a much more formidable opponent."

"So this is just a game to you?"

She gazed at me with eyes as serious as the intent behind all her seeming fun and games. "No, dear, not in the least. I am trying to catch a murderer who killed a woman in cold blood. Even if she did deserve it."

Interesting point of view.

"Did it ever occur to you, dear, that if you had arrived at the house and strolled in a while earlier, and the killer had still been there—there might have been *two* women on the floor with knives in their chests?"

Actually, it hadn't. The car remained an oven, but I felt a chill.

A Trash 'n' Treasures Tip

If duplicates of the same antique begin popping up at a number of shows and fairs, it's safe to assume they are reproductions. Buy one of these, and you're the dupe.

Chapter Nine

Knock 'em Dead

Police Chief Tony Cassato lived in a remote cabin out in the country, about a fifteen-minute drive from Serenity. I say "about" because—although I'd been to the cabin half a dozen times—Tony has never taken the same route when I was in the car with him.

I'd never been certain why his living quarters were only a little more secret than whatever undisclosed bunker they used to keep Dick Cheney in. Maybe Tony was protecting me from accidentally divulging the location during one of Mother's inquisitions. Maybe he was shielding himself from me dropping by unannounced—he obviously valued his privacy. I couldn't say.

As usual, he picked me up in his unmarked car promptly at the designated date time (seven P.M.), and also as usual, I was waiting on the porch, ready to hurry down the steps and hop in the front seat before Mother could waylay him. This I easily accomplished, so easily I suspect Mother was keeping a low profile after successfully pulling off her tape-recorder stunt that afternoon.

With the sweetest little smile, he said, "You look nice," referring to my for-once styled hair, made-up face, and low-cut pastel-floral maternity dress, showing off my swell new swell of bosom. (Might as well accentuate the positive.)

"It's hard not to feel like a cow, at this stage," I said.

"That's bull," he said with a twinkle, eyes on the road ahead, and we fell happily silent for the remainder of the drive.

One of the greatest things about Tony and me was that we could be quiet together—silence was not awkward for either of us; in fact, we welcomed it, after life with Mother (me) and life in a pressure cooker (him).

He took yet another route—I'd been born in Serenity, but he somehow knew the area far better than I—and it was twenty minutes this time before we slowly bumped down the narrow, foliage-chocked dirt lane that led to the cabin.

Tony's dog, Rocky, alerted to our arrival, was waiting on the small wooden porch as we pulled up. To a stranger, the black-and-white mixed breed mutt with a k.o.ed circle around one eye (like the Little Rascals fido), could be taken for a formidable guard dog; but I had gotten to know the canine's true nature: a lazy, lovable, slobbery kisser.

I got out of the car and Rocky trotted up, sniffing me, searching for a tantalizing whiff of Sushi. Since I'd just had a bath and the dress was new, the mutt gave me a "phooey" look, losing all interest, and quickly went over to his master, who was after all retrieving a sack of groceries from the back of the car. Even if I'd carried a whiff of shih tzu, food would have trumped it.

"I'm afraid there's no air-conditioning," he said as we went up the few steps to the porch. "But I'll open all the windows, and there's a nice breeze. . . ."

Indeed, the wind had picked up, rustling the tall pines

surrounding the cabin in a whispered promise of a cooler night.

Inside, a pleasant, woodsy aroma awaited, the place roomier than it appeared from without. To the left as you went in was a cozy area with a fireplace and an overstuffed brown couch, along with a matching recliner; to the right, a four-chair round oak table shared space with a small china hutch. A short hallway led to a single bedroom, tiny bath, and kitchen, with a small porch on the back.

I noticed a certain change in decor immediately.

"What happened to your collection?" I asked, referring to the half dozen or so antiquated wooden snowshoes that had been nailed haphazardly to one wall.

Tony, having set down the bag of groceries, was hanging up his suit jacket and gun-in-shoulder-holster on a peg by the door. "It looked out of season," he said with a shrug. "So I replaced it with my collection of fishing gear."

And indeed he had: antique rods, wicker creels, and nets now graced the wall (also haphazardly). An attractive, slightly older man with a cabin in the woods and a decorative knack. What more could a girl ask for?

I nodded my approval. "The old rubber boot is a nice touch."

He had such a nice smile when he bothered to use it. "Didn't want you to think I'd never hooked anything with that gear—I landed that baby in the pond behind the cabin."

And Mother said he didn't have a sense of humor.

In the kitchen Tony unpacked the groceries (nothing that required a hot oven), and I set the table in the main room, using mismatched dishes from the hutch. While he arranged a variety of cold meat and cheese slices on a platter, I prepared an old family recipe from a list of ingredients I'd provided Tony earlier for his grocery-shopping trip.

DANISH SALAD

1 cup unpeeled, cored, diced apples
⅓ cup blanched almonds, chopped
½ cup mayonnaise
1 tsp. sugar
2 stalks celery, diced
¼ cup plump raisins
¼ cup cream, whipped
White pepper

Combine apples, almonds, celery, and raisins. Mix together mayonnaise, sugar, and whipped cream. Combine fruit mixture and dressing. Season with pepper to taste. Chill.

While we were completing our kitchen tasks, Rocky stood by, ever watchful for spills. Since there weren't any, which was driving the poor pooch bonkers, I waited till Tony turned his back for a moment, then slipped the mutt a slice of turkey.

"I saw that," Tony said.

Cops. He either had eyes in the back of his head, or knew me too well.

"Once you start that," he chided, "he won't let you stop. Fair warning."

As the salad chilled in the small fridge, we made fresh lemonade, using real lemons, sugar, water, and ice.

Dinner was peaceful and pleasant, with the breeze flowing in from the windows, and we kept to safe, crime-free,

Mother-free topics (no sense in getting indigestion), like our mutual interests in movies and antiques.

The aftermath of the meal required little cleanup, and by eight-thirty, we had retired to the couch, Rocky plopping down in front of the fireplace on a tan throw rug, his large head resting on crossed paws, his belly full of the meat and cheese I had snuck him under the table (as he kept nudging my leg with his nose—Tony was right).

But the subterfuge cemented our friendship—Rocky and me were tight now.

And if a man's dog loves you, you are in solid.

I stretched my legs out on an ottoman, kicking off my pink flats, revealing my poor feet, swollen from the heat, not to mention pregnancy. Tony noticed, too, and leaned forward to massage them.

"No Technicolor toes this time?" he asked, referring to my penchant for multiple neon nail polish.

"Not since you made fun of me," I said, faking hurt feelings.

"Don't give me that. You like the attention. Like this . . ." And he ran his thumb along the sole of my right foot.

I let out an orgasmic sigh. This was about as much fun as a seven-month-plus-preggers girl could manage on a hot date. . . .

Finished with the massage, he sat back, put one arm around me, and I leaned my head against his strong shoulder; we stared at the unlit fireplace, where in cooler weather, flames had danced, warming our bodies and our hearts. Somehow the memory of the fire seemed just as warm.

"Tony?"

"Ummm?"

"Can I ask you something personal?"

"Maybe."

"Why do you like me?"

"What kind of question is that? Of course I—"

"I'm not looking for compliments or anything."

He breathed in deeply through his nose. "Well . . . let me count the ways. You have chutzpah—although it doesn't always manifest itself in a good way."

"Oh?"

He nodded. "You can be reckless. But your heart's in the right place."

"Yeah, it is. Right here . . ."

And I placed his hand over a very plump breast.

"Now you're just being mean," he said.

But he left it there.

"Tell me more good things about me," I said.

"Okay. I admire the way you've overcome adversity."

"Like having Mother to deal with on a daily basis?"

"That, and more."

Pause. "Any time you want to say 'pretty,' I think I'm ready."

He squeezed my breast very gently, removed his hand, and kissed the tip of my nose. "That goes without saying."

"No, it doesn't."

"Okay. But you're not pretty."

"No?"

"You're beautiful."

And he kissed me.

To the outside world, he seemed cold; but this kiss wasn't cold. Nor was the way I returned it. When our lips finally parted, he asked, "And what about me?"

"Okay. You're pretty."

He laughed. "I gave it a serious shot. Come on. You, too."

I thought for a moment. "You're intelligent—if a little bullheaded . . . strong, and . . . mysterious."

"But not *really* pretty?"

"No."

"How about . . . handsome?"

"Oh. Well. That goes without saying. . . ."

We kissed again.

Some minutes later, we settled back against the couch, and I broke the romantic mood. Partly I did that because there was only so far and only so many places a make-out session with a thoroughly knocked-up Brandy could go. But also because there was a subject that needed broaching.

"Senator Edward Clark is my father," I announced.

Tony didn't surprise easily. But the only way to accurately describe his expression was "agape."

He blinked and managed, *"What?"*

"I mean, he's my *real* father. As in biological? Mother is really my grandmother . . . biologically speaking. Are you okay? That vein in your forehead is throbbing. . . ."

Tony pulled away enough to look at my face, a wide-eyed questioning look on his.

"It's true," I said with a matter-of-fact nod. "I spoke to Senator Clark just the other day. The senator admits that he and Peggy Sue had an affair the summer she was working on his campaign . . . thirty years ago or so. She got pregnant. You're looking at the result."

I didn't mention that Peg had been seventeen at the start of the affair. He was a cop, after all, and certain uncomfortable statutory issues were better off not explored.

No longer agape, his expression serious, in full interrogation mode, he asked, "Did you hear this from Peggy Sue?"

I nodded. "But only *after* I confronted her—she originally claimed my real biological father was some auto mechanic who died in Vietnam. But it was Connie Grimes who shared that scandalous little tidbit about my birthright."

"How did she tell you?"

"In one of her frequent anonymous letters a few months ago."

He frowned. "Anonymous letters—did she threaten you in any way?"

"Why? Were you thinking of prosecuting her? We'd need a Ouija board. You aren't looking at me like a . . . a suspect, are you?"

"No. Not at all. But please go on. This is information I need to have."

"Okay." I paused, then continued. "I don't know *how* Connie knew about the pregnancy. She worked at that campaign office, too, way back when, so maybe she saw something, heard something, even just guessed."

He was nodding.

"Or figured it out from something Peggy Sue said, either at the time or over the years—hard to believe, but Peg and Connie were friends, ran in the same social-climbing circles. Whatever the case, once Connie knew about me and my real father, that was all it took to send her into high gear and start causing *real* trouble."

I then told Tony about my morning meeting with the senator, who had divulged that Connie tried to blackmail him to keep the information quiet, but that he sent her packing. I realized my father had probably told me this in confidence, and telling the Serenity chief of police about the attempted blackmail almost certainly would have repercussions.

But this was a murder case. And even Connie Grimes deserved to have her murder solved. And her murderer caught and punished. And maybe thanked. . . .

Tony had removed his arm from around me, and was sitting forward in thought. As I had suspected, this information was news to him.

I continued. "Please understand—I'm not trying to cast suspicion on Senator Clark for Connie's murder. I really don't think he had anything to do with it . . . but I'm not so sure about that aide of his—Denise Gardner?"

Tony frowned, glancing back. "What makes you say that?"

"Oh, only her threatening me twice about keeping my mouth shut about my relationship with the senator . . . because of the upcoming election." I laughed bitterly. "I think she thinks this"—I gently patted my bulging baby bump—"was *more* of the senator's handiwork."

Tony's eyebrows went up.

"No, she isn't *that* twisted. . . . I just don't think Senator Clark has shared any of the particulars with her. She did know Connie was trying to blackmail him, but I don't think she knows the details."

"If she thinks the senator is responsible for that"—he looked pointedly at my tummy—"maybe she *should* be told."

I shrugged. "Anyway, I . . . I just wanted you to know that. All of it."

Tony's face turned darkly serious. "You're afraid of the Gardner woman?"

"I don't know!" But the way I blurted that said *yes.* "Maybe I'm just paranoid, or maybe my pregnant hormones are running wild—but sometimes I feel like I'm seeing a killer around every corner."

He took my hand in his. "If it's any consolation, Brandy, we are very close to making an arrest—we just need more evidence. I'm just glad that this time you and your mother are not sticking your noses in . . . her big one and your pretty little one. If you *were*, I'd be worried for your safety."

"Well," I said, with a smile that I hoped was credible, "thank heavens for that. The sooner this investigation is over, the better. You wouldn't want to tell me who your suspect is . . . ?"

"No."

"Even if I promised not to tell Mother?"

"No. She might chloroform you and haul you over to that Tilda woman to hypnotize it out of you."

That made me giggle, but I wasn't entirely sure he was kidding.

"All things considered, though," Tony said, "please stay home—unless you're with *me* . . . you'll be safe then. And if it'll make you feel better, I can have a patrol car make regular swings by your house." He patted the hand in my lap. "But I don't think you're in any danger."

"I . . . I guess I'm being silly."

Of course, later, the real danger would be Mother, kicking me in the shins for not getting out of Tony who he was close to arresting. But at the moment, I was fine not knowing. All I wanted was to sit there with Tony and feel safe.

Darkness had enveloped the cabin. Tony got up from the couch, and turned on a nearby table lamp, throwing a halo of soft light upon our area of the room. He was bending to pet Rocky when the lightbulb popped, running out of its juice, throwing us once again into darkness.

At least, that's what I *thought* had happened.

Tony grabbed me roughly—*didn't he know I was preggers!*—pulling me to the floor in front of the couch, covering me with his body, as all around us came the sound of *snick! snick! snick!* and the shattering of glass and the splintering of wood.

"Keep down," he said urgently in my ear.

Only then did I understand that we were under attack.

The *snicks* were gunfire, silenced gunfire that was no less deadly for its understatement.

Rocky, suddenly alert, fur standing up on his back, poised to growl or attack or maybe even flee, seemed to look intently at his master for which of those to do.

"*Gun!*" Tony commanded. "*Fetch!*"

The mutt flattened himself to the floor, and began to crawl away from us, like a boot-camp soldier slithering through mud. Under other circumstances, it might have been cute; even in those circumstances, it was amazing to see.

From where I lay pinned by Tony, I couldn't see what the dog did next, but after a long while, maybe a whole thirty seconds—the room falling deathly silent after the attack—Rocky crawled back with Tony's gun clamped in his jaws like a big metallic bone.

Apparently, Rocky was not just a lazy, lovable dog free with his slobbery kisses, but highly trained!

"They'll be coming soon," Tony whispered, "to see if we're alive."

They?

Then more than one suspect in the Connie Grimes murder investigation was worried about an imminent arrest! Maybe it was time to tell the chief that Mother and I *were* sticking our noses into his investigation. . . .

Tony reached for the throw rug in front of the fireplace, and when he lifted the rug—to my astonishment—along came the lid of a trapdoor it was attached to.

"We're going down," Tony whispered. He'd grabbed a flashlight from somewhere. "Perfectly safe. Don't be afraid. Feel for the ladder. . . ."

With his help I eased myself into the yawning hole, finding my footing on first one rung, and then the next, finally reaching solid ground. I moved over as Rocky came next, in one big leap, landing safely with a thud, and just the tiniest growl / groan.

Tough critter.

As Tony paused in his descent, I heard a metallic click of a lock on the lid.

Then we stood in total darkness, but for only a moment, until Tony switched on the flashlight, and I could take in our surroundings. We were in a dirt hole about seven feet deep; a low tunnel led off into more darkness.

I whispered, "Here I thought *I* was paranoid."

Of course when bad guys are shooting silenced slugs at you, it technically isn't paranoia anymore.

His whisper was barely audible. "We don't have much time before that trapdoor is discovered." He grabbed my hand, and gestured to the tunnel with the flashlight, its beam light-sabering around. "You'll have to duck. . . ."

With Rocky in the lead, as if he'd performed this drill a hundred times *(had he?)*, we crouched, moving along the narrow tunnel, the flashlight showing the way.

"Where does this go?" I whispered back.

"To my barn. Dates back to Prohibition days. From there we'll have to cut through the woods. Think you're up to it?"

"Do I have a choice?"

"Not really."

"When this is over?"

"Yeah?"

"Let's have a little talk about me being safe as long as I'm with you."

"Fair comment."

In another few minutes we exited the tunnel to a duplicate hole where another ladder awaited our escape.

He took me by an arm and whispered into my ear, "If

they've anticipated this, and I can't do anything about it, I'll do my best to drop the gun back down to you."

What, before he died?

"Tony . . . I'm scared . . . I'm really *scared*."

"You have a right to be. If something happens to me, you'll have the gun, and you just stay down here and make them come to you. You ever shot a gun?"

"Yes."

"Good."

Tony went up the ladder, slowly, quietly, not making a creak. I was probably making more noise than that, just trembling in my clothes. Finally, he opened the exit trap door, popped up for a look around, and . . .

. . . nothing.

No gunfire, no Tony dying, no gun dropping down for me to make an Alamo standoff in the dark with a mourning hound.

Which was nice.

Tony reached down for my hand.

I gave it to him, but whispered, "What about Rocky?"

No matter how well-trained, surely the mutt couldn't jump *up* a ladder.

But I needn't have worried about Rocky—he was right behind me, climbing the ladder like a circus dog. I grinned in spite of the danger.

Then all three of us were crouching on hay-carpeted ground. Just exactly where in the barn I couldn't say, as Tony had switched off the flashlight.

He whispered for me to stay put, then crept to a window to look out. In a moment he was back.

"Let's go," he said softly, and pulled me along in the darkness. I prayed that I wouldn't trip over a metal pitchfork or step on a loose board or otherwise do anything that might give us away.

Then, fast as a jump cut in a movie, we were safely out

a barn back door, running in the woods. Rocky led the way with the aid of an almost full moon that was giving the surreal world an ivory wash. Several times I stumbled on a rock, or tree root, but Tony was right there to catch me, then pull me on. At some point my adrenaline kicked in, and I pulled away from Tony and sprinted like I wasn't pregnant, wasn't even *fat,* not knowing where we were going, just following Rocky's switching tail.

Once, Tony came up alongside me and whispered that we could stop for a rest, but I declined, and we resumed our escape deeper into the forest, the terrain becoming hillier, ivory-touched bluffs visible in the distance.

At last, just when I thought my side might split, Rocky stopped on a dime, up ahead by a grouping of large boulders, then turned with sublime canine patience to wait for the humans to catch up.

"Where *are* we?" I asked, out of breath, feeling safe enough not to whisper now. "Wild Cat Den?"

The terrain looked similar to the state park where I had so often taken Sushi hiking.

Tony, seeming not winded in the least, answered, "Close to it—that part of the countryside, anyway. Look—you can hide here while I go for help."

"But I'm all right," I protested.

The immediate response to that came not from Tony but from my side, where a sharp pain disagreed.

"No," he said firmly. "I can move faster without you. Rocky will stay. I can leave the gun with you."

I was about to ask, "Stay *where?*" when Tony pulled back brush from in front of one of the boulders, revealing the entrance to a cave. Apparently he hadn't taken Rocky and me off running willy-nilly through the night; rather, he'd had a destination in mind.

I guess this was better than me hiding in a hole in the

ground. The whole purpose of this exercise was to avoid winding up in a hole in the ground.

The mouth to the cave was more like a slit in the rock's wall, but still wide enough for a burly chief of police and even a pregnant lady to slip through. Unlike most of the local limestone caves I'd been in—which were too small to stand up in—this was larger, and bigger. I wondered if Tony had altered it, as part of an escape route.

He was saying, "You should be comfortable in here until I get back. You'll have the gun, and I'll give you the flashlight, too—but don't use the flash until I cover the entrance again."

He had taken my arm, depositing me on the ground against the stone wall. "You say you know how to use a gun?"

I nodded numbly.

"The safety is off, and there's one in the chamber, so be careful. Don't shoot any cute toes off."

"Tony?"

He was crouching before me. "Yes?"

"You didn't plan this escape route in case some suspect in a Serenity murder investigation came looking for you . . . did you?"

"No."

"These people shooting at us? They didn't kill Connie, did they?"

"No."

"They're professionals."

"Yes."

"From your past."

He nodded. "I'm sorry, Brandy. I didn't mean to involve you. I didn't think they'd find me out in the sticks."

With hicks like Mother and me.

"This is . . . mob stuff?"

He nodded again. "New Jersey. People I testified against."

So Mother's fabrication about Tony's past was no fabrication at all! What if she had somehow, unwittingly led them to him? She had a kick in the keister coming, just on principle.

A stabbing pain in my stomach hit me like I was the one who'd been kicked.

Tony grabbed my arms. "What is it?"

A lightning bolt racked my body. "I . . . I think I'm . . . sorry to say . . . this . . . don't be . . . mad . . ."

"What?"

"I think I'm . . ."

"Not going into *labor?*"

"Got it in one." I was breathing hard. "You are good."

Tony got to his feet. "I'll be back as fast as I can with paramedics. Rocky, stay!"

At least he didn't say, *Rocky—boil some water!* I don't think I could handle a dog that well trained.

As for me, I wanted to scream, "Don't leave!"

But I knew that it was imperative to get me to the hospital as soon as possible—if the baby was to survive.

So I said, "*Go!* I'll be fine. Just the first contractions. But please do *hurry.*"

But he was already gone.

With the mouth of the cave covered again, I switched on the flashlight for company.

Rocky—commando canine—stood guard next to me, eyes alert, sensing that I was in trouble.

I had to stay calm.

Breathe deeply . . . that's right, through the contraction. Get your mind off the pain. Think of something else. . . .

"*Aunt Brandy? Where was I born?*"

"*In a cave, dear, while mob assassins combed the forest trying to kill us. I had a gun at my side, and for a midwife, there was a Little Rascals dog that could climb ladders.*"

A Trash 'n' Treasures Tip

If you find you've bought a knock-off, and there's no re-course for getting your money back, well, then . . . try living with it. Many reproductions are well made. And you won't feel so bad when you do break it. But if you ever do sell it—don't try to pass it off as the real thing just because *you* got taken. The only thing worse than a fake antique is a genuine liar.

Chapter Ten

Knock Before Entering

I won't go into details about my rescue—how I managed not to give birth before the paramedics arrived, how they had trouble getting me through the narrow entrance of the cave, a sort of birth of its own, and the agonizingly long trip carried on a stretcher over rough terrain, to a waiting ambulance, and then on to Serenity General Hospital.

That's all you get. Living through an ordeal like that once is enough.

I will tell you that I'd barely made it into the ER when the baby arrived—a girl—alive and with all the necessary fingers and toes, to be shuttled off to an incubator, where the little thing began her fight for life.

I was in no danger whatsoever, unless mob hitmen or murder suspects tracked me down, safely tucked as I was into a hospital bed, with Tina and Kevin at my side, joyous at the arrival of their baby and doing a commendable job of not being angry with me for endangering her.

A good thing, too, because I was too weak to put up a defense, as if I had one. I tried not to face the possibility that if the child didn't make it, my friendship with Tina would almost certainly flatline, too.

I felt fairly druggy, and I may have asked it already, but my first memory was asking Tina, "What do the doctors say?"

"Touch and go," Tina admitted, then put on a brave smile and said, "but she's a fighter."

Kevin reached for my hand and squeezed it, firm yet gentle. "We don't want you blaming yourself, Brandy. You could hardly have anticipated this."

I wasn't sure how much they knew, and wasn't sure I should fill them in—Tony being pursued by mob assassins was his business, not mine. Of course, getting chased down an underground tunnel and hiding in a barn and running through the woods and holing up in a cave did sort of make it my business.

But I could only do so much thinking. What I *could* do was feel the tears running down my cheeks.

No, I couldn't have anticipated what happened out at Tony's cabin, but I could have stayed at home and kept a low profile for nine months. Not go on with my selfish life as if it was no big deal a baby was cooking inside me. I tend to cut myself a lot of slack, but if that child didn't make it, I would never forgive myself.

Never.

Somehow it didn't help to hear Tina say graciously, "We knew the risks." She managed a dry laugh. "You don't exactly lead a normal life, do you?"

Kevin added, "But you were our only hope of having a baby together, Brandy, and if—*when*—she's strong enough to come home with us . . . we'll be forever grateful to you."

He was so incredibly sweet to let me off the hook that I started bawling. This did not help, because Tina and Kevin sat there looking at each other uncomfortably. Was there any moment I couldn't ruin? Where did I get this capacity for doing just the wrong thing?

Mother sailed into the room.

And I remembered where.

"I've just come from my prayer group," she announced with self-importance, "and we dedicated a *whole* half hour to the little baby." She looked at my guests. "By the way, what have you decided to call her?"

Tina smiled. "Brandy."

I had just gotten my bawling under control and now *this* honor, after all I'd done. . . .

"Really?" Mother acted like she had tasted something sour, tending to her blubbering offspring by taking a post across the bed from Tina and Kevin, and absentmindedly handing me tissues off the bedstand. "Is that set in *stone,* dear? Because, you know old-fashioned names are making a comeback! Oh, like Abigail, and there's Charlotte, and Ella, even Isabel, and what else? Vivian, possibly."

I smiled, snorting snot. I wasn't sure if Mother was kidding, but I didn't care. She'd made me smile. Even laugh, because that's what that snort had been, mostly.

Kevin grinned at her and said, "We like Brandy."

Mother sighed. "Well, at least it isn't a *made-up* name. When Brandy's name was chosen, it was inspired by a popular song, and it never occurred to me that the little girl was being named after an alcoholic beverage. That kind of thing can haunt and traumatize a tyke and cause them to grow up to be extremely neurotic and willful. Of course, your little girl can always have it changed later if she doesn't like it."

"You know," I said, not smiling as much now, "I *am* right here."

"Yes, dear, of course," Mother said. "I meant in no way to disparage you. . . . How *are* you, by the way?"

"Fine. Thank you for getting around to asking."

Mother clapped her hands and beamed. "I have just

seen the little angel! They had her out of the incubator for a moment, and she is drinking formula like a fish!"

Probably more like a minnow, I thought.

Tina practically leapt from her chair. "Really? Oh, Kevin, let's go see her. Maybe they'll let us hold her for a second!"

In a moment the hopeful, joyful couple had gone, and Mother took one of the chairs.

"Dear," she began, her tone shifting into serious mode, "I'm not clear on what exactly happened on your date with the chief."

So I swore her to secrecy—as secret as Mother could be expected to be, that is—and related the events of last evening.

For a moment, she said nothing—not as unusual for her as you might think, when she was really drinking in the good stuff.

Finally she said, "You know, dear, I *suspected* that Chief Cassato had run into some trouble back East, before he came here."

"I thought you'd just made that up."

"Oh, no. Have you forgotten who the real detective on this team is?"

"Spill."

Mother shifted in her chair. Her expression was an odd cocktail of equal parts pride and chagrin. "Well, dear, on a certain occasion I was left to my own devices in the chief's office alone, and I—quite innocently—stumbled across something."

"You haven't done anything innocent since around 1936."

She frowned, then huffed, "Are you interested in hearing this or not?"

"Yes. Sorry. Didn't mean to disparage *you.*"

Mother straightened, chin high, as if to suggest she was of a noble breed quite incapable of doing anything untoward. "*Quite innocently* I happened upon a letter from the Attorney General's office in New Jersey, warning Chief Cassato about mob retaliation."

Hence the rumor that had circulated around Serenity. And Tony's cabin precautions.

I frowned at her. "Do you realize how dangerous spreading that around was? You could have been the instigator of what happened out at that cabin!"

"I don't think so, dear. I don't think any of the ladies I exchange, uh, news with would likely have any underworld connections. . . . Ah, speak of the devil!"

Tony was entering the room. "Nice to see you, too, Vivian," he said flatly, looking past her to give me a warm smile.

Mother stood and arranged herself like a big bird making sure its feathers were unruffled. "Well, I'm sure you two children have lots to talk about!"

And she departed.

Tony stood at my bedside near where Mother had been seated. "How are you feeling, sweetheart?"

"Pretty good." I smiled, liking the sound of that. "Turns out they have really good drugs at these hospitals. Don't tell the law."

"Promise I won't. When will you be released?"

"Soon as tomorrow, I think. This wasn't near as hard on me as on that little . . ."

I started to tear up.

Like Mother, he handed me tissues. Then he pulled up the chair she'd vacated, and said, "Once you're home, what then?"

"Bed rest for a week or so."

"Think you can sit still that long?"

"Probably not. But right now I feel like I could stay in bed for a month."

His expression turned troubled.

"Brandy," he said, "it's probably unkind to get into this now."

"What?"

"We aren't going to be able to see each other for a while."

Normally, when someone you love—it was *love,* by now, wasn't it?—says those words, it's devastating.

In this case, however, I could hardly argue. He was in a dangerous place in his life, and me being part of it not only put me in harm's way, but made his job all the tougher.

"I . . . I understand. But how long is 'a while'?"

His response was indirect. "I'm taking a leave of absence for a few weeks—to find new lodgings."

"Then you're not leaving Serenity?"

"I don't think so. It's a little up in the air, but . . . I just can't continue to run. But I have no right to involve you, either."

I knew he was right, but I heard myself saying, "Why don't you let me decide that?"

His smile was meant to comfort me, but I could see the sadness in it. "Okay . . . but for now—until the investigation into the attack is complete—we'd better limit it to talking by phone."

"Tony?"

"Yes?"

"What happened to your wife and daughter?"

"Brandy . . ."

"Were . . . were *they* killed?"

He shook his head. "They're safe."

I should have been relieved. Only a terrible person would have preferred to hear that his wife wasn't alive and well. A terrible person who loved him.

"They're in Witness Protection."

"I'm glad."

"We're divorced."

I'm glad!

"My wife never forgave me for putting her and our daughter in danger. I haven't even been able to see my daughter since they went out of my life."

"Don't you have any visitation rights?"

"I can't know where they are. That's the Witness Protection Program for you. We've talked on the phone a few times, under restricted conditions. But that's it."

"That's awful." I meant it.

"I appreciate that. But as far as my marriage breaking up . . . it was for the best."

He stood, strode to the hospital room door, then turned. "I never tried to pass myself off as perfect, Brandy. I hope you know that."

I smiled. "Maybe I should have mentioned that to you myself."

"What?"

"That I'm not exactly perfect."

He smiled, even laughed a little. Blew me a kiss.

And was gone.

Now, it's my duty to admit to you—and to Mother—that while I was bed-bound, I was unable to participate or even anticipate what Mother was doing as a solo sleuth. I had the option of reporting what follows to you in my words, and buffering you from the full-on Vivian Borne experience, or giving her some more rope.

But, as Mother has pointed out, letters to our publisher indicate that readers don't mind spending a little time inside my Mother's lively head. So I am turning half of another chapter over to her.

Understood, Mother?

Half a chapter. . . .

* * *

Dearest ones! This is Vivian with you once more. As Brandy has pointed out, I am sharing this chapter with my darling daughter. But one and a half chapters is better than nothing (although not as good as two, so keep up your letter-writing campaign).

Once again, Brandy's customary way of leading into my section(s) was to include certain disparaging remarks, which I feel emanate from a certain jealousy that the reviews of our nonfiction accounts often seem to single out my chapters for praise.

Perhaps that's why this time she has not included words to the effect that you, gentle readers, should take what I have to say with a grain of salt, adding a disclaimer that she was not responsible for what I write. And to her credit, this time she didn't do that . . . although by mentioning the above, perhaps, inadvertently, I just have.

But I digress.

Where to start?

Our action begins a day after I visited Brandy in the hospital. In the morning, Peggy Sue brought Brandy home, where she (Brandy) was to remain in bed for a few days to fully recover. I am happy to report that the wee one in the incubator was doing splendidly, although the same could not be said about *my* wee one.

I could tell by her lethargic demeanor that Brandy was having postpartum depression, and so I brought the dear girl a Prozac capsule to get her back on the road to blissful mental stability.

(These past months, living with Brandy *off* her medication was stressful for me, to say the least, and hazardous to my own mental heath. Contrary to what Brandy thinks, *I* only take *my* medication to please her, as I really have no need for it.)

Brandy—propped up with pillows, Sushi snoozing contentedly by her side—was asking grumpily, "What am I supposed to do while you're gone?"

I had just informed her that I would be leaving to do a little investigating on my own steam—which was actually more than a "little." In fact I was sure—after listening to the tape recording of Rhonda's hypnosis session—that I knew precisely who Connie's murderer was, and planned to confront the killer.

But I knew it was probably not wise to tell Brandy my plans.

(*NOTE FROM BRANDY:* The last time Mother decided to go out and "confront the killer," she managed to burn down the fairgrounds grandstand.)

(*NOTE FROM MOTHER:* But the killer was caught— see *Antiques Flee Market*—and we now have a splendid new grandstand, although my efforts to have it named after myself were to no avail, though the mayor seemed interested. In fact, he said to me, "I would be delighted to see it called the Vivian Borne Memorial Grandstand." A lovely sentiment from a lovely man.)

(*NOTE FROM BOTH:* But we digress.)

"Well, dear," I said, "you *could* find out if this thingamajig is important."

And, just to keep her occupied and make her feel of some small importance to our investigation, I tossed a little silver disc on the bed.

Brandy frowned. "That's either a CD or . . . a computer disc. Where'd you get it?"

"Why, from Connie's house the morning I was there. It was beside her little laptop computer, actually. I'd put it in a pocket of the housedress I'd been wearing, and had completely forgotten about it, in the hubbub around getting arrested and incarcerated. I only just now rediscovered it."

"Right," Brandy said, frowning in thought. "I brought

your clothes home when you traded them for prison wear. And please don't tell me about your 'fall colors' again."

"I know you don't feel well, dear, but that's no license to be rude."

Brandy was holding the disc in her fingers, as if it were worthy of care. "Well, I *guess* I can take a look at it," she said. "But it's probably nothing."

"If you do decide to pop it into your computer, be careful getting out of bed. If you feel woozy, get right back under the covers."

"I will." She seemed distracted by the silver disc.

"Very good, dear. Well, I'm off. Toodles!"

"Yeah, right. Toodles."

I hurried away, before Gloomy Gusina could dampen my spirits. Sometimes depression can be contagious, you know, and I certainly had no desire to catch it from her, like a common cold.

The trolley-car-converted-to-gas was a little late arriving at its scheduled stop a block from the house, which I attributed to the current driver, who was actually a reinstated *former* driver.

Maynard Kirby—a retiree from the fish hatchery—once upon a time had taken the job when his wife lost their (actually his) retirement money on the *River Queen* gambling boat, inspiring him to seek a new occupation. As luck would have it, however, Mrs. Kirby hit the jackpot with her (his) last dollar, and Maynard once again went into happy retirement.

It took many months for Mrs. Kirby to gamble away her new jackpot winnings, but now, finally, Maynard found himself back behind the wheel of the trolley, again pursuing his late-in-life new career.

Climbing aboard, I gave Maynard—a bespectacled gentleman with salt-and-pepper hair, and matching trimmed beard—a curt hello. No need to waste time buttering him up for special treatment, as the two places I wanted to go were downtown, and already on the regular trolley route.

The trolley was half full and I found my way to a vacant seat near the back, settling in.

I will now finally finish the amusing story about Billy Buckly—the town's famous little person, whose grandfather was a Munchkin in *The Wizard of Oz*. I began telling the tale in *Antiques Flee Market* (another reason to buy that one, if you haven't already!), but at the very end of my chapter, Brandy—who was holding me to a strict word count—cut me off in midsentence! Talk about your serpent's tooth!

Then, in *Antiques Bizarre* (collect them all!), I tried once again, only to be hampered a second time by that blasted word count. I know the publishers are trying to save trees, but honestly, can one little paragraph more matter that much? I suffer this indignity only because Brandy is the one signing the book contracts, which she says makes her "the boss."

So, here, at long last, is my trolley story. One day a summer ago, Billy Buckly had been sitting on my lap—not out of amorous intentions but due to a shortage of seats—when the trolley inexplicably braked. Well, little Billy flew through the air as if he'd been shot out of a cannon (we were in front, facing the back of the bus), and he landed on the lap of recently widowed Mrs. Snodgrass. She took him home to tend to his bruises, and consequently, they fell in love and got married.

(I'm afraid with all of the build-up, my story might not seem that funny. Perhaps you had to be there. But one can't help but wonder if Billy had begun on Mrs. Snodgrass's lap, and wound up in mine, might the story have had a different and more satisfying ending? Brandy with Billy Buckly as a stepfather—now *that* would be entertaining!)

Again, I digress. Last time, this time, I promise.

Now, on to my investigating. . . .

I disembarked the trolley at Pearl City Plaza, and went inside the antiques mall, where I had arranged for Cora Vancamp to meet me. Barring any traffic accidents on her part, she should arrive shortly. In the meantime, I checked on our booth, to see what if anything had sold since Brandy and I were last there.

Disappointingly, all our merchandise appeared present and accounted for—I'd been hoping that at least Brandy's foolish purchase, the silly yellow smiling clock, marked down to a ridiculously low two dollars, would not be grinning back at me.

But it was.

So I picked the thing up and marched over to Ray— busy as usual at the center checkout counter—and tossed the clock on the counter.

"I'll buy this," I said.

Ray, bent over another antiquated sewing machine, looked up, stared at me, then at the clock, then back at me again.

"You've made a mistake, Vivian."

"I think not."

"But it's *yours.*"

"Of course it is," I snapped. "But I don't know of any other way to get rid of it. Besides, it'll cheer Brandy up seeing that it sold—she's confined to her bed, you know, since the baby was born." I dug in my purse. "Here's ten dollars."

Thoroughly befuddled now, Ray picked up the clock. "It's only marked *two.*"

"I am well aware!" Some of these older people are *so* obstinate!

I handed an engraving of Alexander Hamilton toward Ray. "Record that the clock sold for ten—if she asks, tell her two people were fighting over it, upping the price. The girl is just gullible enough to believe it, and she'll think she made a profit on her misjudgement."

Who said I didn't have a heart?

(*NOTE FROM BRANDY:* Does she think I don't read my own books?)

The bell over the front door tinkled, announcing a customer, and I looked over to see Cora, wearing another avian dress—yellow hummingbirds, on this occasion. She stood tentatively, beady eyes flitting behind her glasses searching futilely for yours truly, even though I wasn't more than twenty feet from her.

"Over here, dear!" I called. "Follow my voice. . . ."

Blind as a bat, the poor thing, but without the radar.

Cora hurried over, hauling a small cardboard box that she placed on the counter among the sewing machine parts.

"Ray," I said, "I understand that you had a chance to get a gander at Cora's Acklin clock shortly after Harry bought it—is that not correct?"

Ray's forehead creased in puzzlement. "Yes. Back then I was working part-time for Ben Timmons. Harry wanted to know how to care for it."

I opened the box, then withdrew the clock. "Is *this* the same Acklin?"

Ray reached for the clock, then gently pushed aside some sewing parts, and set it before him.

I expected Ray to take several minutes before he answered, but in less time than it takes to remove a girdle, the elderly gentleman said, "No."

Cora's little eyes grew large. "But you didn't look at it *closely!*" she protested.

His gaze was kind but firm. "I didn't have to, Cora. After all these years, I know a knock-off when I see one . . . and that's a knock-off—stem to stern."

"But . . ."

"Years ago, Harry brought your clock in to me at my old repair shop, for a cleaning, before he gave it to you. It was one of the finest examples of an Acklin bedside clock."

Cora began to tear up, poor old baby. "Then . . . then what *happened* to my clock? Where is *it?*"

"Now, now, dear," I said, handing her a tissue. "I think you *know* what happened—Ben Timmons switched it with this one. He lied to Brandy and me that you'd been swindled, and sold a fake clock. But as Ray has said, it was very real. Authentic."

"I don't understand," Cora said. "He lied to you . . . he switched clocks on me . . . ?"

"Yes. Exactly *when* is unknown, but almost certainly he did so after your eyesight began to fail, and he thought that you wouldn't notice the difference."

Cora wiped her eyes with a tissue. "How ever am I going to get the real one back?"

I gave her the reassuring smile of a true heroine. "Not *you*, dear, *me*. *I'm* going to retrieve it for you—wherever it is. There are laws against selling stolen property!"

I whipped out my cell phone.

Darn—deader than disco.

Now I ask you, people, I am no Luddite, but how am I supposed to remember to charge the blessed thing all of the time? Is it a phone or a camera battery?

I looked at Ray. "Be a dear boy, and give the police a jingle. Tell them I'm heading over to Timmons Clock Repair."

Ray said, "If Timmons is guilty of theft and fraud, we should just send the police over there. You have no business getting involved, Vivian."

"I solved the crime, and I will nab the miscreant."

The old boy just smiled at me. A lopsided smile at that. "Really, Viv?"

"Yes. I intend to make a citizen's arrest!"

How to make a citizen's arrest:

1) If possible, notify the police in advance. Try to time it so that they show up just *after* you've made the arrest. (Otherwise, they'll get all the glory. And you might get throttled or even shot, since criminals are by nature untrustworthy.)

2) Evaluate the situation carefully. To avoid being sued for slander, be absolutely certain that a crime has been, or is being, committed. (Or in my case, fairly certain. Almost certain. Pretty certain.)

3) When stopping a person in the act of an illegality, announce, "Stop!" (If the perpetrator has a gun, however, you might prefer to just run.)

4) Inform the "perp" (short for "perpetrator") that you are making a citizen's arrest. (Otherwise, he might just think you're daffy.)

5) Call the police, if you haven't already. While you wait for them, remember that you are not allowed to forcibly restrain the perp. (Tripping him, however, might be acceptable.)

6) When the police arrive, identify yourself (in my case, an unnecessary step), and tell them what you have witnessed or what evidence you have obtained.

Leaving Cora behind with Ray and her knock-off clock, I hoofed it three blocks to the old funeral home, arriving at the repair shop somewhat winded.

On the door, a plastic WE'LL BE BACK AT clock-face sign had its hands set for noon—which was in fifteen minutes. Apparently Timmons was taking an early lunch, or was out making a delivery.

Rather than cool my heels, I decided to make a preemptive strike (as they say on CNN) and backtracked to the vintage clothing store located in the adjacent funeral parlor.

Nodding a friendly hello to the young saleslady at the cash register, I plucked a 1940s blouse with shoulder pads off a rack, then sailed into a makeshift dressing room, disappearing behind the 1950s boomerang curtain.

After arranging the blouse on a chair, I exited out the back of the curtained dressing room, hurrying to a door connecting the parlor to the embalming room / clock repair shop. If you are wondering how I knew this, write it off to reconnaissance.

The old door had an ancient lock, and one swift bump with my hip (not the artificial one!) was all it took to push through. I stepped into a room used for storing business materials—mailing cartons, paper, packing materials, and the like.

Quicker than you could say "citizen's arrest," I was around the counter, moving past the embalming tables, and heading into the back room, where the clock parts were kept. My only apprehension was that Timmons might also know the rules of citizen's arrest and arrest me for breaking and entering. But one must take one's chances in the investigatory game.

What I was looking for was evidence that that persistent rumor was true: a supply of Acklin clock parts had survived the fateful fire of 1920.

And I struck gold, almost immediately. Opening a large metal cabinet revealed various shelves on which were Acklin pearl-shell clock faces, gold hour and minute hands (I slipped a set in my pocket), finely crafted cases, and precision inner workings. But other key parts were missing, making it impossible for a complete Acklin to be assembled from what had been salvaged from that long-ago fire.

This explained why Timmons was plundering other Acklin clocks from trusting customers (including Brandy and me)—substituting fake parts, and sometimes (as in Cora's case) complete timepieces . . . which allowed him to put together and sell the *real* if Frankenstein-assembled thing, for a tidy sum.

"Something I can help you with, Vivian?" a voice asked behind me.

Startled, I whirled.

Ben Timmons was smiling, but there wasn't anything friendly about it.

For a moment I was flummoxed, almost as bad as when I went up on my lines in *I'm Getting My Act Together and Taking It on the Road.*

But cool customer and consummate performer that I am, I quickly recovered. "No, Benjamin, I think I've *found* what I was looking for. . . ."

And casually, I expounded my case against him. It wasn't until I was nearly finished that I noticed the antique rubber embalming hose that he brought out from behind his back, clasping the ends with both hands, drawing it taut, like a rope.

This was, I admit, disconcerting.

I immediately combined steps three and four. "*Stop!* I'm making a citizen's arrest! I've already called the police, and they'll be here any minute. So if you have any notion of killing me—"

The hose went slack in his hands. "I'm not going to kill you, you old busybody!" he said. "Not that I wouldn't like to, and they'd probably give me a gold medal and a parade for it."

That was certainly rude.

He took a step forward with the hose. "You broke into my shop. That's against the law—I'm going to tie you up until the police *do* get here."

So the possibility of making his own citizen's arrest *had* occurred to him.

I put my hands on my hips. "*If* you're making a citizen's

arrest yourself, you can't tie me up. I refer to step four—no restraining. Anyway, I don't *believe* you. . . . You're going to kill me just like you did Connie Grimes!"

"What?" He was both surprised and alarmed. "I didn't kill that stupid woman!"

"But I *know* you did . . . and so do the police. A witness saw you go into her house the morning of the murder, and then come running out. Just try to deny it!"

Did I fail to mention to you, darlings, that I had heard this on Rhonda's hypnosis tape? I won't apologize, because both Agatha Christie and Rex Stout do that sort of thing all the time.

And I also didn't mention to *Timmons* that the witness in question was a convicted felon whose hypnosis testimony, however helpful to a skilled investigator like yours truly, would not hold up in court.

The clock expert let the hose slip from his hands to the floor.

Stalling for time until the police arrived, I said, "Connie knew what you were doing, didn't she? And threatened to expose you, or perhaps sue. Maybe she even tried to blackmail you—that was that terrible creature's style, after all. So you went over there to discuss her terms, and when she wasn't looking, you took a knife from the kitchen and—"

"No!" Timmons blurted. "I *didn't* kill her! All right, I admit I've been stealing Acklin parts from my customers . . ."

How wonderful! Just like a witness breaking down on the stand in *Perry Mason!* I could just imagine the court reporter getting all of that down.

". . . but I didn't kill that woman, Vivian. I swear it. She was *alive* when I left!"

"So that's your story, is it?" I said with a smirk.

Since the police had still not arrived, I bent my head and spoke into my cleavage.

"Did you get that, Chief? Benjamin Timmons admits stealing from his customers for his own personal gain!"

Timmons asked astonished, "You're wearing a *wire?*"

"Of course, you poor misguided soul . . . you don't think I'd confront a *murderer* without properly accessorizing!"

"I told you, Vivian, I didn't kill her! It's the truth."

"So you claim," a deep male voice said.

Officer Lawson stepped in from the embalming room.

"You sure took your time!" I huffed.

Brian handcuffed Timmons, reading the man his rights, then led his prisoner out, through the embalming room.

"I led him to believe I was wired," I said proudly, trailing behind.

Brian looked back with half-lidded eyes. "Vivian—you're *permanently* wired."

"Why, thank you, dear boy."

After everything I'd done for them on so many cases, it was nice to get a compliment from the police for a change.

Mother's Trash 'n' Treasures Tip

Knock-offs can hurt the value of the genuine article if enough of them infiltrate the marketplace to make collectors wary, especially in cases where the knock-offs are so well made that they can fool the well-trained eye. Even I have been known to make such mistakes, as when I mistook a reproduction chamber pot for the real thing. I thought it looked suspiciously clean.

Chapter Eleven

Knock-out

After Mother had gone off to do her sleuthing, I decided I was tired of resting. I really didn't feel that bad—I had some aches and pains that were no worse than a mild flu, and anyway, they were knocked back by the painkillers the doctors had thoughtfully prescribed.

Besides, as all females know, the best way to feel better is to look better. So—to the slumbering Sushi's dismay (she looked up at me with her spooky eyes and her expression said, "Is this trip necessary?")—I eased out of bed, trundled into the bathroom (free to trundle again!), took a nice long warm (not hot) shower, put on a little make-up, let my damp hair dry naturally, then found some of my old summer clothes that fit—tailored tan walking shorts, a red-and-tan plaid blouse, and simple white Keds.

Want a quick, free getaway? Take some of those hotel toiletries you always swipe, currently gathering dust in a bathroom closet, and use them for your morning bath ritual. *Suddenly, you're transported back to Le Meurice, the Savoy, or the Ritz-Carlton.* (Or in my case, the Peoria Super 8).

After a simple breakfast of orange juice and cereal, which settled nicely, I wandered into the music / library room, which was crammed with the musical instruments and books that Mother keeps buying at garage sales and flea markets. Quite honestly, it didn't smell so good in there.

No one in our family that I ever heard about was musically inclined, although Mother claimed she used to entertain returning local WWII servicemen by performing "Boogie-Woogie Bugle Boy of Company B" on the cornet. But once when I handed her one of her flea market trumpets and asked for a demonstration of her gifts, it sounded more like "Boogie-Woogie Bugle Boy of Company B-*flat*."

The room was now the Music / Library / Incident Room, because, in addition to the dinged and dented musical instruments, and moldy, tattered books, Mother had dragged in an old wooden classroom chalkboard on rollers, which she used to keep track of her latest murder investigation.

(Migod, had it had gotten *that* bad? Was I now accepting, ever so casually, the reality that one murder investigation would be followed by another, and another . . . ?)

Anyway, written on the board in pink chalk, apropos to the current investigation, was the following:

DENISE GARDNER / SENATOR'S AIDE—
9:10 A.M. entered front. Left 9:35 A.M.
BEN TIMMONS—
9:50 A.M. entered front. Left 10:10 A.M.
TINA—
10:20 A.M. No entry. Left 10:25 A.M.
BLUE MINIVAN (DRIVER UNKNOWN!)—
10:30 A.M., Seen in driveway. Left?
VIVIAN—
11:05 A.M. entered. Left 11:35 A.M.
BRANDY / SUSHI—
11:45 A.M. Entered back (found body).

Apparently these notes were culled in part from the secret tape Mother had made of Rhonda's hypnosis session. And to me it seemed clear that Ben Timmons had killed Connie Grimes—otherwise, who would have let him in the front door?

But then, Mother said the front door was unlocked when she arrived (I hadn't bothered to try it), so it *was* possible that Denise Gardner had done the deed, and Ben Timmons invited himself in (as Mother had), saw the body, and fled.

The blue minivan (mistaken by Mother as Peggy Sue's) might be explained as innocently as some lost soul using the Grimeses' driveway to turn around.

Shrugging, I went back upstairs to my bedroom, where I kept my computer, and fired it up.

Soosh was on the covers, on her back, spread-eagled, as the room was beginning to get warm, the central air unable to keep up with the outside heat. Her little tongue was lolling.

I slipped the computer disc Mother had confiscated into the computer drive, and opened it, assuming it would contain nothing important, yet hoping it might.

Unfortunately, as I had expected, the files were a bunch of junk—Christmas letters, mailing lists, recipes, tax information. The typical things found on anybody's home PC.

But one file caught my interest—labeled "SWAK," the universal shorthand for "sealed with a kiss"—and I opened it.

Sure enough, it was a love letter, written last month to "My dearest darling." This was, of course, none of my business. Didn't the deceased deserve a little privacy?

Not on my watch. Not on a murder investigation (the *current* murder investigation), and not from a woman (AWOL from her sick bed) who shared DNA with Vivian Borne.

And as I continued to read the single-spaced one-page

letter, I got more and more intrigued. From the e-mail's contents, it became apparent that Connie had been having an affair, and that funds she had been gathering (by blackmail?) were being socked away for the lovers' future life together. The salutation was "Forever yours." Wasn't that a candy bar? Fitting sign-off for Connie Grimes.

One passage, however, did seem especially curious. "Soon you will understand my motives, darling, and we will be together always, living in the lap of luxury, and you will never have to slave away again."

That made me wonder—was it possible her affection was not being reciprocated? Or that a once-attentive lover had called it off? Because there seemed to me to be a desperate edge to the letter, an almost hysterical tinge, as if Connie were trying to convince a once (and she hoped future) lover of her actions.

Suppose Connie's paramour had been Ben Timmons? And the real reason she was angry with him that morning at the clock repair shop had nothing to do with an overcharge (as Timmons had claimed). Had the clock fixer either dumped her, or rebuffed her advances?

Interesting questions. But who could confirm or deny this theory besides the principles? Then it came to me—if anyone might know of the affair, it would be Peggy Sue!

Even though it was the morning of Peg's weekly country club bridge game, I thought I could catch Sis alone when she was the dummy, or in the tank, or rubberized, or whatever it's called—I don't pretend to understand the game, nor do I understand why anybody's still playing the dumb thing in the twenty-first century. (No letters, please! I have a right to my opinion.)

I intended to leave Sushi behind, placated with a doggie treat, but when she heard the jingle of the car keys, she had a hissy fit, barking and hurling herself at me like a furball kamikaze. Evidently she felt neglected these past few days, with me in the hospital, and Mother out and about.

I warned her, "It's hot outside—you won't like it." But the words (Sushi understood "hot" and "outside") failed to dissuade her.

From experience I knew that if I left Soosh alone, she might well apply her sharp little teeth to one of my expensive leather shoes. And if there's anything sadder in life than a chewed-on Stuart Weitzman, I haven't encountered it yet.

So from the front closet I retrieved the leopard tote with the pink boa feathers that made her sneeze, and rather than strap on a hot dog (hold the mustard) to my chest, I just placed Sushi in it, and hauled her and myself out to the un-air-conditioned car.

I was feeling good. You can't *prove* that I doubled my pain-killer dosage before I left.

Thankfully, the country club was only minutes away, and soon Soosh and I were entering the modern, sprawling, tan-brick building, through fancy etched-glass front doors into a cool (temperature-wise, anyway) octagonal lobby, with its formal carpeting, golfer landscapes, and mahogany furniture.

Mrs. Crumley—who, thanks to a wealthy husband, never had to do a lick of work in her life, and who bore a general contempt for any who had—was the self-imposed country club gatekeeper on bridge mornings. The hefty middle-aged woman, who possessed short lacquered hair that bullets could bounce off of, gave me a frown as I approached the small secretariate desk, at which she sat.

"You can't bring that creature in here," she said, waggling a finger Sushi's way, like she was scolding the animal for existing.

"Of course I can," I said. "The dog is blind—I'm her

seeing eye person." I lifted the tote. "Haven't you ever heard of having a license to carry?"

One would think women of leisure would have plenty of time to cultivate a sense of humor, even if they hadn't been born with one. But Mrs. Crumley didn't find me the least bit funny, as she continued surveying us disapprovingly. Here's an interesting question—how can somebody sitting down still look down her nose at you?

Finally she said, "All right, Ms. Borne. I understand you are Peggy Sue Hastings's sister, but that carries little weight. That . . . *thing* can't go any farther than where you stand *right now*—we have rules here, you know." She paused. "What is it you want, anyway? *You* are not a member."

I found a smile. "I can dream, can't I?" I hadn't put any sarcastic spin on that at all, but I kind of wondered if Mrs. Crumly would have noticed if I had. "I'm here to see my sister. Who is a member, as you pointed out."

"Well, she's playing bridge and can't be interrupted."

Now I made an apologetic face. "I know, I'm so sorry— but this is an emergency."

She sighed heavily. "Oh, all right . . . I'll see if she can come. . . ." The woman stood. "Why don't you people stop *bothering* her during bridge club—first last week, then this week! Doesn't she deserve a respite like anyone else?"

What was she talking about?

Mrs. Crumley had come around the desk to face me, standing with hands on expansive hips. Some of the boa feathers tickled Sushi's nose and the pooch sneezed, sending canine spittle flying upward toward the woman's heavily made-up face.

I suppressed a smile. *Score one, Sushi!*

Mrs. Crumley wiped her puss with a paw. She *hummped.*

"At least your sister's *husband* knew enough not to interrupt the game."

Well, of course not. Mild-mannered Bob wouldn't have a confrontation with anyone, least of all this Cerberus at the gate.

Mrs. Crumley disappeared down the carpeted hallway in the direction of the dining room, where the bridge games were held. And in less than a minute, Peggy Sue came hurrying toward me, typically lovely in a cream-color wrap dress with a handkerchief hem that I recognized from Donna Karan's summer line. Like I said, I can dream, can't I?

"What is it, Brandy?" Sis asked, alarmed, out of breath. "What are you doing out of bed!"

"I'm fine," I assured her. "I'm just getting a little exercise."

"Exercise!"

"Peg—please. I need to ask you something important."

"What?"

I pulled her over to the etched-glass doors, out of earshot of Mrs. Crumley, who had resumed her station and was staring from behind the desk at us.

I whispered, "Do you know if Connie ever had an affair? Particularly lately?"

Peggy Sue's concern morphed to annoyance. "*That's* your 'emergency'? You're not *still* looking into her murder, after all that has happened to you? Putting that baby at risk wasn't enough? Now you have to endanger your own health?"

I ignored all that. "*Was* she having an affair?"

Peggy Sue sighed. "I don't know. Maybe."

"Maybe? You want to be a *little* more specific?"

Reluctantly, she played along. "Just a feeling. She seemed so happy—for *Connie*, anyway . . . in light of the fact her husband was cheating with his secretary."

"Connie knew about that?"

Sis shrugged. "Everybody knew. But Connie didn't seem to care."

Sushi was getting heavy, and I switched the tote to my other hand. "Could Connie have been carrying on with Ben Timmons?"

"Who? The clock repairman?" Sis laughed. "Whatever would make you think *that?*"

"He has money, doesn't he? Owns his business."

"That doesn't mean he isn't in debt up to his you-know-what."

Like Bob.

"Anyway, isn't Ben Timmons gay?" she asked.

"I don't know. Is he?"

"I always thought so. He's not married."

"Which automatically makes him gay?"

"No, of course not. But gay or straight, he certainly isn't the kind of man Connie would have gone after. A clock repairman working out of an old funeral home? Please. *You* knew Connie. *You* know the type. A real social climber."

My jaw would have dropped if that lack of self-insight on my sister's part hadn't already frozen my face.

"Connie Grimes had a husband with a respectable job. She'd been around the car business long enough, Brandy, to know *not* to trade *down.*"

Mrs. Crumley snapped, "Mrs. Hastings! Please don't keep the other ladies waiting!"

Sis touched my arm. "Sorry, honey. I've got to get back to the game."

As I watched Peggy Sue disappear back down the hall, it occurred to me her husband might be more helpful than she'd been. Since he'd partnered his insurance agency with an investment brokerage, Bob might be just the person to find out for me whether Connie had been investing large sums of money. If not with him, then some other firm. Couldn't he place a few calls—one agent to another?

Seemed worth a try.

Since expanding his business, Bob had moved his operation from a strip mall on the outskirts of town to the old five-story First National Bank building downtown on Main Street, purchasing the white-stone Grecian fortress and saving it from demolition, forever buying Mother's gratitude.

This was my first trip to Bob's newly remodeled digs—not exactly having a lot of cash lying around to invest, nor needing new car insurance on a vehicle that was probably already technically totaled. By the time the Buick putt-putted into the spacious parking lot, Sushi was whimpering from the heat, regretting the jaunt with me.

"You need to learn more words," I advised her.

Her fuzzy face said, *Huh?*

I wasted no time in entering the old bank, the former lobby transformed from a stodgy, cold, gray-marbled teller area to a warm, inviting waiting area with all the comforts of an expensive family room.

To the left were matching overstuffed couches and chairs arranged around a huge flat-screen TV (turned to the business channel, of course), positioned above a modern fireplace. To the right were Internet stations, and a coffee bar with several canisters of hot java, pitchers of ice water and lemonade, plus complimentary fancy cookies and scones.

Free grub! Brandy likes. I poured some water into a cup and let Sushi lap it, while I stuffed a frosted cookie in my mouth, already beginning my post-baby diet.

A directory on the wall said Bob's office was on the top floor, so I caught an elevator up. As I got off, an attractive thirty-something black woman with sleek chin-length hair stepped from behind her desk to greet me. Her short peach cardigan over a ruffled silk cream blouse, with a short brown tiered skirt, was likely J. Crew. See, I am a detective.

"I'm Sheila," she said pleasantly. "May I help you?"

"Ah, hello, Sheila—I'm Brandy . . . Bob's sister-in-law?"

"Oh, yes." She smiled, showing off perfect white teeth. "Bob has mentioned you often."

I didn't ask whether in a good way or bad. Friendly as she was, she had a dignity and faintly formal air that made me feel like I was wearing clown shoes. From J. Crew, natch.

Shelia's eyes went to Sushi in the tote. "I approve of your accessory."

And her stock went up with me ten points. Here less than a minute, and investing already. . . .

"Thanks," I said. "Any chance I could I get in to see Bob? I guess you know I don't have an appointment, but it's kind of important."

She nodded to the nearby closed door. "Mr. Hastings *is* rather busy—he's been in there all morning working on reports. But I'll be glad to ask. A break might do him good, and I can't imagine him turning his favorite sister-in-law away."

That was sweet, but then I was also his only sister-in-law.

Sheila returned to her desk to use an intercom. "Sorry to interrupt, Mr. Hastings," she said, "but Brandy Borne is here to see you. . . ."

There was a pause on the other end, then, "Send her in."

She turned to me, saying, "He'll see you," as if I hadn't heard Bob's reply.

Why do they always do that?

I crossed to the door, opened it, and stepped inside.

The large room—formerly the dreary bookkeeping department of the bank (I'd worked there one summer during community college)—had been transformed into what seemed more a modern loft apartment than an office, complete with a living room area, conference / dining table, kitchen, and work space.

Which made sense for Bob, since he spent so much time at the office.

"Wow," I said. "Impressive digs."

Bob—casually if expensively attired in a light blue polo shirt, tan slacks, and brown leather slip-ons with tassels—stood in the middle of his fiefdom.

"Brandy, how are you? I'm surprised to see you out and about so soon. How is the baby?"

He gestured for me to sit on a couch that faced a fabulous view of the river—once a row of small windows, the wall had been replaced entirely with glass. Sliding doors led to a narrow, decorative-but-functional balcony to allow a closer inspection of the passing riverboats and barges.

"The baby is doing really well for a preemie," I said, settling on the leather couch, Sushi in the tote on my lap. "And I'm fine. Drugged to the gills, but fine."

He smiled at that. "Good to hear mother and daughter are doing well." Bob settled into an overstuffed chair across from me, a modern glass coffee table displaying business magazines between us.

We exchanged some more small talk, and when that petered out, Bob asked, "To what do I owe this visit?"

From my shoulder bag I withdrew a printout of Connie's letter, saying, "I won't tell you how I got this, but I'd like you to read it. I think you might be able to help me find out who was responsible for what happened to Connie."

I put the paper on the glass table, and Bob reached for

it. He read for a moment, his face impassive, then suddenly he set the paper back down.

I read into his quick, stoic reaction that just a glance had been enough to tell him the letter was distasteful or intrusive, and I said, "I could summarize it if you like."

"No. That won't be necessary."

"Have I said or done something wrong? I was hoping you could help me."

He stood, crossed to the glass wall, then looked out over the panoramic view. "It's not that, Brandy. It's that I already know what it says."

It took me a moment to process that. "You're not saying that it was . . . was written to *you?*"

Bob glanced sideways and nodded, his back still to me.

"Then you . . . and *Connie*. . . . ?"

He laughed harshly, then turned. "Oh, it wasn't mutual. That woman was delusional—insanely jealous of Peggy Sue. I don't even think she was really in love with me. She just wanted everything Peg had—house, money, cars, vacations, friends . . . you name it. And that extended to me." He paused for a moment. "When Connie somehow found out that Peg had had a baby out of wedlock and told me . . ." He shrugged.

A baby out of wedlock: me.

"You hadn't known, before?"

He shook his head. Hands went into his pants pockets. "It wouldn't have mattered. I love your sister." His eyebrows shot up. "I guess it's 'mother,' isn't it? Seems obvious now. How could I not have known? I'd have been there for you, Brandy, better than I ever was. I always liked you. As far as Peggy's concerned, well . . . I guess you know I'd do anything for her."

Anything?

My neck began to tingle.

He seemed to be talking as much to himself as to me. "When Connie threatened to go public with the information, I offered her money for her silence."

I said, "I think she may have been blackmailing others, like my father, Senator Clark. And possibly Benjamin Timmons, who may be involved in some kind of fraud with his customers."

"I wouldn't be surprised if Connie hadn't been bilking them and more. She was a spider caught in her own web. She told me she'd been investing that money for the time when I would leave Peggy Sue for her. But when the money no longer placated her, when I could no longer keep her at bay . . . she gave me an ultimatum." He spread both hands. "Don't you see? I couldn't have Peggy Sue hurt. My girl, my sweet girl, dragged through the mud like that . . ."

Mrs. Crumley's words came to mind. *"At least your sister's husband knew enough not to interrupt the game."* Secretary Sheila had said that Bob had been in his office all this morning, but I bet she couldn't say that about the morning of last week's bridge club. It must have been then—the morning Connie died—that Mrs. Crumley spotted Bob in the parking lot.

I said, "You switched cars with Peggy Sue, didn't you? Knowing she would have an alibi."

"Yes," he sighed. "My sports car was too recognizable, so I took Peg's, parking mine in the same spot at the country club, then retrieved it later. Don't look so stricken, Brandy. Somebody had to do something about Connie Grimes. More than just shove her in a department store."

I felt sick to my stomach—worse than any morning sickness.

"Don't feel bad, Brandy. You're not putting the final nail in my coffin. Connie had already done that, by having me named as the beneficiary of the investments *and* her life insurance policy. It's just a matter of time before I'll be charged."

Bob was Tony's suspect.

"Oh, Bob, I'm so sorry. . . ."

He smiled sadly. "I know. You've always been very sweet to me, Brandy. Much as I love her, Peg could use some of your qualities—your sense of humor, your heart."

"What now?"

"Nothing good. Listen, uh . . . Peggy Sue's going to really need your support now. When she finds out what kind of financial shape I'm *really* in . . . and not just because Connie had been draining me . . . anyway. Be a good sister. Good daughter."

"I'll try."

"I guess I'd better call your friend, Chief Cassato." Bob moved to his desk. "But first I need to give Sheila some instructions."

He spoke into the intercom. No answer. He tried again. No Sheila.

Bob looked at me. "She must be in the copy room at the end of the hall—would you go down and get her for me, please?"

I nodded, picked Sushi up, and numbly made my way to the closed door.

The next minute I relive over and over in my mind. Did I suspect that Bob only pretended to use the intercom? Did I realize he was purposely sending me out of the room?

No . . . firmly no. Never. But maybe . . . maybe a little bit yes. . . .

In slow motion I open the door of his office. I step out, close the door. But Sheila is there—she looks up from her desk. I turn and hesitate a heartbeat before I open the door to the office again. The sliding glass panels to the balcony stand open. Beyond, the water sparkles as if blanketed with diamonds, while a white barge chugs lazily up river. Just another tranquil day in Serenity.

Bob's office is empty.

Then five stories below, a woman starts to scream.

A Trash 'n' Treasures Tip

One way to spot a knock-off is if the item doesn't show wear and tear where it should. There should be marks around drawer handles, on chair arms or table legs which would be consistent with normal use. If an antique looks so new that it seems too good to be true . . . it *is* new, and it's not true.

Chapter Twelve

Hard Knock Life

Predictably, Bob's tragic demise sent most of the family into a stunned depression. But Mother swung into action, and within twenty-four hours, not a living soul in Serenity hadn't heard that Vivian Borne's despondent son-in-law had taken his life because he had Creutzfeldt-Jakob's Disease. (I think the "fine folks" at Wikipedia had a hand in Mother's affliction selection, too).

This fatal condition (had Bob actually contracted it) would have caused blindness and loss of movement and memory within one year of its diagnosis. And, as she told all and sundry, Mother felt certain Bob didn't want to become an emotional and financial burden to his family, which made his decision "courageous." This was one of Mother's finest performances, and she really did do Peggy Sue and Ashley (and Bob's memory) a service.

Mother's defense of Bob seemed to me particularly gracious in light of the fact that he had not come forward when she was arrested, to clear her of the murder he'd committed. I like to think that while he might have allowed Vivian to go through with a trial—figuring (rightly) that she would likely enjoy the theater of it—Bob fully intended to step up and clear her, should she be found guilty. After all, someone else standing trial for the murder might be enough to muddy things so that he could get away with his crime.

I doubt Mother had thought any of that through, though, and acted less out of compassion for Bob and more out of protecting her eldest daughter.

Perhaps Mother could forgive Bob, but I wasn't sure I ever could. I had thought I'd known the man—he'd seemed sweet, kind, even mild-mannered, but he had stabbed Connie Grimes to death with a kitchen knife. Whatever homicidal fantasies I had ever harbored about that dreadful woman, such a savage act was beyond my comprehension. Sometimes still waters do run deep. And scary.

Sis had her own forgiving to do. After the funeral—a small, private affair—a numb Peggy Sue, who had never been one to worry about finances, got a rude awakening when she learned just how far in debt her late husband had sunk them: double mortgage on the fancy house and loans on three cars, with the recently expanded business severely overextended.

Bob had even cashed in his hefty life insurance policy to keep them afloat (although, with his suicide, the company wouldn't have paid out, anyway).

In anticipation of Peggy Sue having to sell her house in the near future and move in with us, Mother readied the guest room. We had plenty of space in the house, but not enough beds, so I rounded up an air mattress for Ashley in case she might visit from college.

On the brighter side (yes, Brandy was back on Prozac, so everything had a brighter side now), Mother received a suspended sentence for her interference in Connie's murder, which remains on the books as unsolved. I know for a fact (because Tony told me during one of our lengthy phone conversations) that Sheriff Rudder had pleaded with the judge for leniency on Mother's behalf.

"Well, that was generous of him," I'd said, "considering everything she's put him through."

"Oh, don't misread it," Tony's voice said on the other end of the line. "She deserved a year in the county jail. But having your mother as an extended guest at his facility was nothing Rudder could abide. In fact, he threatened to resign if she were allowed back in his jail."

Mother's suspended sentence, however, came with community service, and she wasted no time in creating her jail theater program, so the sheriff got stuck with her anyway. Whether that's poetic justice or karma (good or bad), I'll leave to you.

In fact, on a recent Saturday evening at the jail, an original play written and performed by the female inmates, and directed by Mother, had its gala opening night (or as gala an opening as a play presented inside a detention center could have, anyway). Mother had invited me to watch the dress rehearsal, going to the trouble of clearing it with the sheriff himself, but I declined, not wanting to spoil all the fun.

I say "fun" not because I was expecting to have a fine time seeing a wonderful evening of skilled amateur entertainment. No. We've discussed before that I am not a perfect human being, and one of my flaws included an ability to perversely enjoy Mother when she was caught up in a complete theatrical debacle.

There was no guarantee of that—Mother had been genuinely good at times, particularly when she wasn't directing herself. But the odds were in my favor, particularly with this surefire combo of elements—Vivian Borne and the Cell Block H Players? I was almost giddy with anticipation—there's nothing quite so entertaining as seeing Mother fall flat on her face.

Was that really so terrible of me?

Don't answer.

The performance was being presented in the women's common room at the jail, and at seven o'clock—one hour until curtain time (though there wasn't a curtain)—deputies began herding attendees through the main floor metal detectors, then escorting them (four at a time) through the various security doors, and finally depositing them in rows of plastic chairs, borrowed from our church.

The audience—approximately fifty to sixty people, carefully selected and approved—included the mayor and his wife (Mother calling in a favor for having helped to elect him), several city council members, four of Mother's Red-Hatted League gal pals, Tina and Kevin, Judith Meyers from NAMI, the senator's aide, Denise Gardner (of all people), and of course various family members of the cast. The latter included a fairly rough element, but they were dressed in Sunday clothes and on their good behavior. Maybe they were hoping for an early release.

Absent were Senator Clark (who was back in Washington), Peggy Sue (in seclusion and anyway not up to it), and the chief of police (still on leave until Monday). I'd been hoping Tony would come, because I hadn't seen him since he'd stopped by my hospital room. Several phone calls, yes, but nothing in person. . . .

The stage at one end of the room was small, consisting of risers borrowed from the high school, and the scenic direction simple, the only props being five plastic chairs placed in a row. Next to the stage, on the floor, was a large game wheel with an arrow, its pie-shaped sections each sporting a word, "REGRET," "HAPPINESS," "SHAME," "LOVE," and so forth.

There was no program pamphlet. Mother detested printed programs and whenever possible withheld them from her audiences, disdaining anything that might take the audience's eye off of her or her production. Once, when she was playing Lady Macbeth, a woman in the front row was so engrossed in her program booklet, rustling the pages, that Mother paused mid-Bard to walk to the footlights and declaim, "Madam! I am about to die. You might not want to miss it."

(Lady Macbeth dies off-stage in Shakespeare, but Mother's interpretation has her dying on stage. She once explained, "I find that audiences always enjoy my death scenes, dear," to which I could only comment, "It is a crowd pleaser.")

While Mother had kept this, her first penal play, under wraps, she *had* told me that the format was unusual: one act, free-form, and in part improvisational. I say "in part" because, knowing Mother, she would not leave everything to chance.

I was sitting toward the back (so I could watch people's sure-to-be-amusing reactions), next to Tina, who had baby Brandy strapped inside her oversized shirt, up against her skin.

Have you heard about the new procedure for preemies called "kangaroo care?" If the baby is otherwise healthy, he / she could go home as long as the infant remained attached to the Mother's warm chest. Anyway, so far it has worked for Tina and Kevin.

(*Admission:* If you think it's easy to give birth and then hand the baby off to someone else—even a dear friend—think again. While it gave me joy to see Tina with little Brandy, I couldn't see that sweet small creature without my heart swelling with pride, and then breaking a little.)

At precisely eight P.M. (according to the white-faced, black-handed institutional clock), a security door to one side of the stage opened, and five female inmates in their orange prison jumpsuits filed in, with Mother—dressed like a gypsy—following behind.

Wow, I thought. *A gypsy! This would be rich. . . .*

The inmates walked up the few steps to the stage, took their chairs, while Mother assumed her position on the floor in front of the big wheel.

I recognized the women from what Mother had told me about her short incarceration—young, blond, slender Jennifer; stocky crew-cut Carol; tall, curvaceous red-haired Sarah; dark-complected, pudgy, curly-haired Angela; and the only one I'd seen before, the woman who'd given the hypnosis testimony—brown-haired, attractive if hard-featured Rhonda.

One odd (but I think interesting) side note: Carol was due to be released for her assault charge days before the performance, but she had shoved poor jail deputy Patty just to get her sentence increased. (I don't know if this was Mother's idea or Carol's. But I suspect Mother of aiding and abetting.)

The ceiling lights dimmed.

I contemplated clapping, so that Mother would be assured of *some* applause, but no one else seemed so inclined.

The room fell silent, and you could hear the proverbial pin drop, though I had a feeling if one did, a guard would go for a gun. Suddenly a spotlight fell on Mother (I wondered if they were using the same one usually reserved for third-degree-type interrogations).

"Come one, come all!" gypsy Mother called, like a flamboyant circus barker. And wasn't this a circus, after all?

She gestured to the round prop. "Come spin the wheel of fortune!" (I would have to remind Mother that she might be open to a lawsuit from the popular game show, should she, as promised / threatened, take her play out on the prison circuit.)

Mother pointed animatedly to Mrs. Hetzler, an ancient

gal pal in the front row. "You, madam—come forward and spin the wheel!" I suspected Mrs. Hetzler was a shill, to get the ball rolling (or wheel spinning).

The former high school English teacher, who had given me a "D" on my essay final for bad composition (readers who pause here to say, "I'm not surprised!" should be ashamed!), stood uncertainly and took the few steps to the wheel.

Now frail and stooped, her navy pantsuit looking two sizes too large, Mrs. Hetzler had trouble giving the wheel a good whirl, and I wondered if it had to go all the way around to qualify, like in *Match Game* reruns.

Apparently not, the arrow quickly pointing to the word, "SHAME."

As Mrs. Hetzler returned to her seat, Mother turned ever so slowly toward the stage. "Who among you feels shame?"

The spotlight shifted from Mother to the seated inmates. Like in BBC's *Whose Line Is It, Anyway?*, the women looked briefly at each other, then Sarah stood, and strode to the edge of the stage.

Looking out over the audience for a moment, she said, "My name is Sarah Coulter, and a year ago I had everything going for me. . . ."

I was impressed with her casual manner as she told of her road to the county jail; yet her tale of woe—freely admitting her guilt—was neither maudlin nor self-serving. Once Sarah seemed to lose her train of thought, but the women behind her uttered words of encouragement, and she finished her frank monologue to loud applause.

A second audience participant was selected to spin the wheel, followed by another inmate performance, and so on; sometimes the monologues were lengthy, other times short. And not all the admissions were downers. Humor peppered throughout to lighten the mood, as when Rhonda came forward with the word, "REGRET," and said what she really regretted was getting caught. Everyone laughed at that (well, not everybody—Sheriff Rudder seemed less than amused).

I thought the format of the play was very clever: each woman had a story ready for each of the possible words that might come up, and yet it was spontaneous as to which word was landed on, and who felt like taking it. Brilliant.

But it was Carol who stole the show, when she came forward when the wheel stopped on "LOVE."

"I think I first knew I was different was when I was in middle school. I told my mom about it and she promised she wouldn't tell Daddy, but she did. He whupped me for it. He said I was trash, but I knew he was trash for hitting me. That's when I left home. I had to live on the street and it was hard. If that wheel stopped on 'SHAME,' I wouldn't talk about being gay, because I'm not ashamed of it. I'm not proud of it, either. I just am. And I know that for all the stupid choices I made in my life—and bein' here in the county jail sure shows I made my share—I know my partner will stand by me. Because she loves me."

No matter how the audience felt about alternative lifestyles, there wasn't a dry eye in the house (yup, even the sheriff).

After the performance ended—to a standing ovation—I had never been prouder of Mother . . . nor more ashamed of myself for looking forward to her making a fool of herself. *I* felt like the fool. I felt like going up there, spinning that wheel to "REGRET" or maybe "SHAME," and telling that audience what a lousy daughter I could be.

After the performance, while the audience was milling, offering their congratulations to Mother and the cast (the guards keeping a watchful eye), Denise Gardner approached me. She was wearing a pale green pantsuit, her bloodred lips and nails replaced with a softer shade of pink.

"Well, that was . . . interesting," the aide said.

Feeling magnanimous in light of Mother's success, I said, "Thank you for coming, Denise."

"It wasn't exactly my idea," she said, intimating that my father had something to do with it. "But I did want to see you again and, well . . . apologize for jumping to the conclusion that you and Senator Clark—"

"Forget it," I cut in. *Really* feeling magnanimous.

She went on. "In my defense, the anonymous note the Grimes woman sent said only, 'I know about the pregnancy.' The senator never clarified that, said he wouldn't 'dignify it.' So naturally I, uh, well . . . Any time you want to let me off the hook, that would be great."

"I was kind of enjoying watching you dangle," I admitted. "You know, Denise, we might be seeing each other from time to time, so it would be better for my father if we made an effort to get along."

"By that, do you mean you'll be going public with your relationship to the senator?"

I gave her a hard stare. "Being somebody's kid isn't a 'relationship,' except in the biological sense. Which is the only kind of relationship I have with him right now."

"I didn't mean to sound quite so blunt. But *are* you coming forward?"

"That's up to him. You might put a little more faith in the common decency of people. Not *everyone* is trying to bring him down. Now if you'll excuse me, I'd like to congratulate the cast."

And I left her to contemplate that.

Monday afternoon, I decided to surprise Tony by dropping in on him at the police station. The back-from-leave chief would have had the morning to settle in again at work, and he should be happy to see me in the flesh after a month of phone-call-only contact.

I took special care getting ready, wearing a new fall out-fit—DKNY dark-washed jeans, tan blazer over a crisp white shirt, and brown-suede Pliner loafers. A girly pink Betseyville shoulder bag offset the preppie look.

Soon I was heading out the door (leaving Sushi in Mother's care) and hopping into my burgundy Buick. The oppressive August heat had changed to cooler September days, and some of the leaves were already beginning to turn bright yellow, burnt orange, and ruby red. Fall was my favorite time of the year, the season that represented the waning, bittersweet years of one's life, seeming more sweet than bitter to me at the moment. But maybe that was the Prozac.

At the station, I asked the female dispatcher if I could see Chief Cassato, so I was pleased when the ponytailed woman with glasses said, "Yes. He said you might try to see him today—I'll buzz you through."

The hallway—normally alive with office sounds—seemed unusually quiet. As I passed by the break room, Officer Munson, eating a late lunch at the table, didn't acknowl-edge my glance. Was he pretending not to see me?

Suddenly I wondered if word had gone round the sta-tion that Bob had most likely killed Connie, and there wasn't anything they could do about it. And I was this loose end blithely invading their territory.

But I wasn't about to let that thought dampen my mood. I intended to make a commitment to Tony today, and tell him how much I'd missed being with him, that I wanted to go forward with our relationship, danger be damned. Or anyway darned. And it was on this lofty cloud that I sailed into Tony's office.

Where I found Officer Brian Lawson seated behind the chief's desk.

At first I thought Brian was filling in for Tony, out on an investigation; then I noticed Brian's personal photos framed and on the desk.

"Brandy," he said, glancing up from paperwork. His smile seemed tentative.

And I knew.

"Tony's . . . He's not coming back, is he?"

"No," Brian said softly.

"Ever?"

"That I don't know."

"Where is he?"

"That I don't know, either." He shrugged. "Witness Protection Program."

My legs felt weak, and I found a chair.

Brian opened a desk drawer, withdrew an envelope, stood, then came around the desk. "The chief asked me to see that you got this. . . ."

I took the envelope and opened it.

I read enough to realize that it shouldn't have been addressed "Dear Brandy," but "Dear Jane."

I refolded the single sheet and slipped it back in the envelope, saving the rest for a more private moment.

Brian put a gentle hand on my shoulder. "I'm sorry, Brandy, really sorry. If there's anything I can do—"

"I'll be fine," I said, a little too defensively, as if trying to convince myself. "Thank you for offering."

I stood and faced him, his puppy-dog brown eyes laced with concern.

"You know I *do* care about you, Brandy."

I summoned a smile. "I know. You're a good friend, Brian."

He put a hand on my shoulder. "There was a time when I was more than that. Can you remember back that far?"

"It's . . . uh . . . not quite the right timing for *that* kind of reminiscing."

Brian nodded. "I understand—as long as *you* under-stand. . . ."

"I do."

"If you need me. Just call."

"Thanks."

In my car, in the parking lot, I finished reading the letter, in which Tony confessed that he loved me, saying that he would return some day—*if* he could "safely settle things" back East.

But he would understand if I didn't wait.

Driving home with the windows down, the cool, fall air blowing my hair around, I thought about all the crazy adventures I'd been through since moving home fifteen months ago; they seemed so improbable. Even impossible.

And if the impossible could happen, so could the possible. Tony could come back one day. Suddenly, I felt hopeful.

I was at another crossroads in life. Where would it take me? Not to mention Mother and Peggy Sue (and Sushi), and assorted other eccentrics here in Serenity.

You're welcome to come along for the ride.

A Trash 'n' Treasures Tip

When buying an antique or collectible over the Internet, protect yourself from knock-offs by making sure the site has a good return policy and positive feedback from other customers. You want to always be able to get your money back on a knock-off. But remember—if you read a whole book and don't like it, there's no money-back guarantee!

About the Authors

BARBARA ALLAN

is a joint pseudonym of husband-and-wife mystery writers, Barbara and Max Allan Collins.

BARBARA COLLINS is one of the most respected short story writers in the mystery field, with appearances in over a dozen top anthologies, including *Murder Most Delicious, Women on the Edge, Deadly Housewives* and the bestselling *Cat Crimes* series. She was the coeditor of (and a contributor to) the bestselling anthology *Lethal Ladies,* and her stories were selected for inclusion in the first three volumes of *The Year's 25 Finest Crime and Mystery Stories.*

Two acclaimed hardcover collections of her work have been published—*Too Many Tomcats* and (with her husband) *Murder—His and Hers.* The Collinses' first novel together, the Baby Boomer thriller *Regeneration,* was a mass-market bestseller; their second collaborative novel, *Bombshell*—in which Marilyn Monroe saves the world from World War III—was published in hardcover to excellent reviews.

Barbara has been the production manager and / or line producer on various independent film projects emanating from the production company she and her husband jointly run.

MAX ALLAN COLLINS has been hailed as "the Renaissance man of mystery fiction." He has earned an unprecedented fifteen Private Eye Writers of America "Shamus" nominations for his Nathan Heller historical thrillers, *True Detective* (1983) and *Stolen Away* (1991). A new Heller novel, *Bye Bye, Baby* will be published in 2011.

His other credits include film criticism, short fiction, songwriting, trading-card sets, and movie / TV tie-in novels, including the *New York Times* bestsellers *Saving Private Ryan* and *American Gangster,* which won the Best Novel "Scribe" award for excellence in tie-in writing.

His graphic novel *Road to Perdition* is the basis of the Academy Award–winning Tom Hanks film. Max's other comics credits include the "Dick Tracy" syndicated strip; his own "Ms. Tree"; "Batman"; and "CSI: Crime Scene Investigation," based on the hit TV series, for which he has also written six video games and ten bestselling novels.

An acclaimed, award-winning independent filmmaker, he wrote and directed the Lifetime movie *Mommy* (1996) and three other features, including *Eliot Ness: An Untouchable Life* (2005). His produced screenplays include the 1995 HBO World Premiere *The Expert* and *The Last Lullaby* (2008).

Max's most recent novels include *You Can't Stop Me* (written with Matthew V. Clemens) and *The Big Bang* (completing an unfinished Mike Hammer novel from the late Mickey Spillane's files).

"Barbara Allan" live(s) in Muscatine, Iowa, their Serenity-esque hometown. Son Nathan lives in St. Louis and works as a translator of Japanese to English, with credits ranging from video games to novels.